THE
MIDNIGHT
LIBRARY

THE CAT LADY

LOOKING FOR DAYLIGHT? KEEP DREAMING.

THE MIDNIGHT LIBRARY CONTINUES....

———

VOICES

BLOOD AND SAND

END GAME

THE CAT LADY

LIAR

SHUT YOUR MOUTH

THE MIDNIGHT LIBRARY

—

THE CAT LADY

DAMIEN GRAVES

SCHOLASTIC INC.

New York   Toronto   London   Auckland   Sydney
Mexico City   New Delhi   Hong Kong   Buenos Aires

SPECIAL THANKS TO
ALLAN FREWIN JONES

—

ISBN-13: 978-0-439-89391-6
ISBN-10: 0-439-89391-7

Series created by Working Partners Ltd.
Text copyright © 2006 by Working Partners Ltd.
Interior illustrations copyright © 2006 by David McDougall

12 11 10 9 8 7 6 5 4 3 2 1   7 8 9 10 11 12/0

Printed in the China
First printing, February 2007

Welcome, reader.

My name is Damien Graves,
curator of that secret
institution:

The Midnight Library.

Where is The Midnight Library, you ask?
Why have you never heard of it?
For the sake of your own safety, these questions are better left
unanswered. However . . . as long as you promise not to reveal
where you heard the following (no matter who or *what*
demands it of you), I will reveal what I
keep here in my ancient vaults.
After many years of searching,
I have gathered the most terrifying
collection of stories known to
humanity. They will chill you to
your very core, and make
the flesh creep on your young,
brittle bones. So go ahead, brave
soul. Turn the page. After all, what's
the worst that could happen . . . ?

Damien Graves

THE
MIDNIGHT LIBRARY:
VOLUME IV

Stories by Allan Frewin Jones

———

CONTENTS

THE CAT LADY

THE CAT LADY

"Scaredy-cat! Scaredy-cat!"

The taunting voices rang in Chloe Forrester's ears as she pedaled furiously down the alley that divided the new housing development from the old part of town. Her cheeks burning, she sped along between the high wooden fences until she reached the big open field known locally as the "Old Green."

Chloe shouted defiantly back to Heather and the rest of the gang: "I'm not scared! I just don't want to do it!"

"Chloe's a big coward!" Heather called.

"Coward!" Maggie and Emma shouted in unison, taking their cue from Heather.

1

"Shut up!" Chloe shouted. "Just shut up!"

Hayley and Megan took up the chant. Now the whole gang was yelling at her. "You're a coward! You're a coward!"

Chloe pulled on the handlebars, lifting herself off the seat to boost the bike up over the curb and onto the grass. She pressed down hard on the pedals, struggling to keep up speed on the incline. At the crest of the round grassy hill, she brought her bike to a halt and turned around to look back. She was thirteen years old, tall and slim with corn-gold hair and a pale, freckled face — except that right now her cheeks were flaming red and her blue eyes stung in the chilly wind.

It had all started when Heather had dared Chloe to throw pebbles at the Cat Lady's windows and then run off. She had refused. Then Heather had called her a scaredy-cat and she'd ridden away, humiliated and angry.

Chloe watched as Heather and the gang rode their bikes to the end of the alley. Heather said something to the others, and they all brayed with laughter. Chloe's cheeks burned with embarrassment — Chloe knew they were laughing at her and she hated it.

As she stared down at the jeering gang, she found herself wishing she had never distanced herself from Tina. Things had been so much simpler when she and Tina had been best friends.

The rift had begun a couple of months ago — due to a stupid fight over a T-shirt. Chloe had borrowed it from Tina for a party, and when she gave it back, there was a stain on it that wouldn't come off. Tina said the T-shirt had been perfect when she had lent it to Chloe — but Chloe was convinced that she hadn't stained it. Neither one would back down.

Chloe had stormed off, telling Tina she never wanted to speak to her again. Then, to make Tina jealous, she'd started hanging around with Heather and her gang, partly because everyone thought they were cool — but also because she knew that Tina didn't like them. She thought that they were all stupid sheep — blindly following Heather. Chloe didn't like Heather much: She was sarcastic and cruel — and she was a bully, too. But Maggie, Megan, Emma, and Hayley were OK. Except for the way they always did everything Heather told them to do. That often got really annoying.

Chloe stared back down the way she had come. The new housing development stretched out, all neat, clean, and orderly in a big crescent to the left side of the Old Green. To the right sprawled the grubby, old industrial part of town. An alleyway was the dividing line between the old and the new. It was paved and had fencing along both sides. To the left, fancy wooden doors led into the yards of the new development, and to the right were an older, battered set of fences — decrepit and entwined with vines and long, spiky-looking weeds. It seemed to Chloe as if the people who had put the fences up didn't want anyone from the one part of town getting into the other.

Not that it stopped the cats! There were plenty of cats. They came mostly from Mrs. Tibbalt's house, a shabby place tucked away behind the fence that bordered the alleyway on the old part of town. Mrs. Tibbalt was a little strange. She was known locally as the Cat Lady. Sometimes Chloe and the gang would look over the tall fence into her garden full of cats. And sometimes Heather would bang on the fence and shout to scare the animals. Chloe didn't like that — she thought it was mean.

The Cat Lady

The Cat Lady's house was a sanctuary for what seemed like hundreds of cats. They were everywhere. Black cats and tabby cats, ginger toms and calicoes, fluffy cats and scraggy cats, young cats and old cats — from sleek and skittish kittens, all gleaming eyes and needle-sharp claws, to ferocious and curmudgeonly old bruisers that hissed and showed their broken yellow teeth at anyone who came near.

For as long as Chloe could remember, there had been dreadful stories about Mrs. Tibbalt.

Tina had first told Chloe these stories, years ago, when Chloe's family had moved into the neighborhood.

"It's true — it's really true," Tina had told her, wideeyed, on that first day at school. "The Cat Lady *kidnaps children.*"

Chloe had not been convinced. "Why would she do that?" she had asked.

Tina's voice had dropped to a whisper. "She takes them down to her cellar and grinds them up to make cat food," Tina had said. "How else do you think she manages to feed all those cats of hers?"

Chloe had stared uneasily at her. "I don't believe it!"

Tina had laughed. "Ask anyone!" she had said. "But you'd better watch out. If you go near her house, she'll come shuffling out and she'll offer you candy to get you to go inside. Then, once you're in there, she'll give you a suspicious drink that will make you feel all sleepy and weak."

"Then what?" Chloe had asked, her eyes widening in alarm.

"Then she'll drag you down to her dark and smelly cellar," Tina had said. "And your head will go bump, bump, bump on the stairs. And you won't be able to do anything about it. She's got this huge old machine down there — like a giant blender. And you'll be lying there helplessly while she turns it on. And it will start clanking and churning — and you'll see a big grinding screw begin to turn way down at the bottom of the funnel. And then the Cat Lady will lower you really slowly into it, feet first — and the worst part will be that although you can't move, you'll still be able to hear the grinder draw closer and closer!"

Chloe hadn't really believed that the Cat Lady turned children into cat food in her cellar, but all the same she had always kept a watchful distance from the house. The Cat Lady didn't come out very often, but when she did, Chloe would watch her warily as she hobbled down the street, leaning on a thick cane, all shrouded up in a heavy, moth-eaten old coat and kerchief. And even after all these years, Chloe still crossed the street to avoid going too close to her house.

A little while ago, she had confessed this to Heather and the gang.

"I know she's just a sad old lady," she had told them. "And I know the stories about her aren't true, but she still gives me the creeps."

Heather had mocked her. "That's pathetic!" she had said. "What are you — six years old?" The others had joined in laughing at her, though Chloe was sure that most of them were scared of the Cat Lady, too.

"You need to grow up a little," Heather had said. "I know how to cure you of being scared of the Cat Lady." She had mounted her bike. "Come on, everyone. Let's go have some fun."

"What kind of fun?" Chloe had asked quickly.

"We can throw stones at her front door for a start," Heather had said. "That would be hilarious!"

"I don't want to do that," Chloe had said. "What's the point? It's just mean."

"Suit yourself, scaredy-cat," Heather had said, laughing as she rode off.

The others had followed her, leaving Chloe standing there all by herself. She had been angry at Heather for making fun of her, and irritated by those four stupid girls who followed Heather around like a bunch of zombies. She knew that Tina was right about them, and this made the feelings of isolation and loneliness far worse. She had felt her stomach turn upside down, and hot tears had prickled behind her eyes, though she was determined not to cry.

And now she was in the same position again, alone on top of the Old Green while the rest of the gang made fun of her.

They're idiots, she told herself as she stared down at them. *But if I don't do what they want they're going to make my life a complete misery.* She frowned. *I'm going to put a stop to this once and for all,* Chloe resolved, and she turned her bike around and rode back down the grassy slope.

"Look, everyone! Scaredy-cat's back," Heather mocked.

"What does scaredy-cat want?" Emma chipped in.

Maggie piped up as well. "You should run home to Mommy, Chloe," she said. "The Cat Lady might get you!"

"Oh, shut up," Chloe snapped.

"Or what?" Hayley said. "You're brave all of a sudden."

Chloe ignored her. "I'll take your stupid dare," she said, looking straight at Heather. "It's no big deal. I just think it's totally pathetic."

Heather looked slyly back at her. "You have to go in through the gate," she said. "Right into the front garden."

"Whatever," Chloe said, trying to sound as if she couldn't care less. *I'll make it look good, but I'll miss the window and aim for the wall,* she thought. "I'll do it once," she said to the group, "but never again. It's totally pathetic and immature."

Heather stared at her, and Chloe met her gaze for a moment. "OK — if you do it right." A slow grin spread over Heather's face as she looked around at the others.

"Did I tell you all about the time I went inside the Cat Lady's house?" she asked.

"You didn't!" gasped Megan.

Heather nodded. "Yes, I did," she said. The others gazed at her in awe. "She'd gone out shopping and she'd left the front door open. So, I decided to go in and have a good look around."

"What was it like?" breathed Emma.

Heather looked at Chloe. "Disgusting!" she said. "It was all dark and stinky and really filthy. Every single room was filled up with big moldy heaps of old newspapers and magazines tied up with string. And there were supermarket bags full of garbage — and black plastic bags with more junk spilling out of them. And there were opened cans of cat food all over the place. And the whole place reeked. It smelled like the cats were using the whole house as one big toilet."

There were squeals and wails of revulsion from the rest of the gang, but Chloe suspected that Heather was making all this up just to freak them all out.

Heather continued her ghastly story. "The carpets were all sticky and squishy underfoot," she said.

"And the wallpaper was hanging off the walls in strips where the cats sharpened their claws. There were cats everywhere! And they were all staring at me, and some of them hissed at me — but that didn't bother me. If any of those monsters had gotten anywhere near me, I'd have given them a good kick!"

"But the Cat Lady might have come back and caught you!" gasped Hayley.

Heather eyed her. "So what?" she said. "What's she going to do? I'm not afraid of her." She glanced again at Chloe — rubbing it in. "Then I went upstairs," she continued. "I found her bedroom. Only she doesn't have a real bed like a normal person. There was just a big, round wicker basket on the floor, with dirty old blankets in it. That's where she sleeps. And there was a great big box of cat litter by the side of the bed." She gave the others a meaningful look. "And it had been used!"

Maggie's eyes widened. "You don't mean . . . ?"

Heather nodded. "It was her toilet!"

There were yells of revulsion from everyone but Chloe.

"That was so disgusting that I just turned around and left right away," Heather said. "The whole place made me feel sick."

"I don't believe it can be that bad," Chloe interjected. "No one could live like that! And I don't believe for a minute that she sleeps in a basket!"

Heather shrugged. "See for yourself," she said. "I know what I saw." She gave Chloe a taunting look. "So, when are you going to go?"

Chloe looked defiantly at her. "After school tomorrow."

Heather smirked. "We'll be waiting."

"I'll be there," Chloe said. She pushed down hard on the pedals and rode her bike quickly down the long alley that led to her home. She was well aware that Heather was probably badmouthing her to the others and saying that she wouldn't turn up.

Well, this time Heather was wrong.

But all the same, Chloe felt a just little bit shaky as she cycled along. Mostly she was angry about Heather and her moronic gang, but there was also a small part of her that really wasn't looking forward to what she had agreed to do the next day.

The Cat Lady

It was a dull, cloudy, and drizzly afternoon as Chloe pedaled away from school and into the old part of town. She turned a corner into the street where Mrs. Tibbalt lived. She saw Heather and the others standing there with their bikes on the other side of the road, waiting for her.

Chloe cycled up to them and stopped.

Heather stepped forward. She was holding something in her hand. It was a chunk of rock — about the size of her fist.

"This is what you're going to throw at the Cat Lady's window," Heather said.

Chloe stared at the big rock. "You said pebbles!"

Heather shrugged. "So? It's a *big* pebble," she said. She glanced at the others, who nodded at her. "We've all agreed," Heather began, "that if you want us to stop picking on you, this is what you have to throw at the Cat Lady's window. But it's up to you, of course. You can always chicken out."

Chloe knew that a rock that size would smash any window it was thrown at. She looked from face to face. They all had the same nasty, eager expression. If she refused to throw the rock, the taunts would start up again. If she agreed, they'd get a big kick out of the Cat Lady's window being broken. Either way, Chloe knew right at that moment that she hated and despised the whole bunch of them.

But she couldn't back out. It was too late for that.

She took the rock out of Heather's hand.

"Throw it really hard," Heather said with a mean sparkle in her eye.

Chloe propped her bike at the curb. The rock felt huge and very heavy in her hand. Without saying a word, she turned and walked across the street. She just wanted to get it over with.

The houses were shrouded by tall evergreen trees, and it was gloomy and dank under the dripping branches. Mrs. Tibbalt's house was set back from the cracked path behind an overgrown mess of hawthorn bushes. Chloe stared through the spiky branches — trying to catch a glimpse of the old woman through the dirty windows. But it was too dark. She peered out from under her hooded jacket, the cold rain pricking her skin.

She could feel the others watching her as she came

up to the broken wrought-iron gate. It hung at an angle from the brick gatepost. On top of the post was a damaged and mottled stone cat. And there was the iron silhouette of a standing cat on the gate, its outlines eaten away by rust.

Chloe edged past the gate. She took a deep breath and looked along the weedy gravel path to the old house. To one side, she noticed a rickety old shed, half hidden under the trees. As always, the house was in darkness. She looked at the gray bay windows. She tiptoed a little way along the path, avoiding the nettles, watchful and listening.

She paused for a moment, looking down at the rock. It was black and jagged — she guessed it must weigh over a pound. She glanced over her shoulder. She could hear a distant hissing coming from the gang — an indication of how they would behave toward her if she chickened out.

She turned back to the house. She clenched the stone in her fist. She lifted her arm up and drew it back, getting ready to throw — aiming for one of the smaller side windows — feeling really bad about herself.

The gauze curtains moved. Chloe froze, her heart

beating hard. Through the grime of the window, she saw a black cat's face staring at her with luminous green eyes. A second cat came and sat alongside the first, its face mottled brown and gold, its eyes yellow.

They were watching her.

She couldn't throw the rock at that window — the cats would be hurt by the broken glass. Then more cats appeared at the other glass panels of the bay window — until every grubby window had watchful faces staring out with yellow eyes, green eyes, and golden eyes.

Chloe heard a rustling behind her. She guessed that it was Heather and the others, creeping up to the fence to watch.

Her thoughts raced wildly as the cats gazed out at her. "I can't!" she breathed. Then she heard again the mocking hissing from beyond the fence. If she didn't throw the rock, the gang would never let her forget it.

She took a deep breath, trying to calm the frantic beating of her heart. The cats stared at her. She swallowed hard. She brought her arm right back and threw. But she deliberately aimed low, in order to miss the windows.

The heavy chunk of rock crashed through the tall weeds under the windows.

There was a dull, sickening thud and a horrible yowl of pain as the rock hit something hidden in the weeds, followed by a sad murmur.

Chloe stumbled forward, her stomach tightening into a ball of dreadful shock.

She saw a small cat lying against the wall in a strange, unnatural position with its head horribly twisted. The rock was close by.

Chloe felt sick and dizzy. She was afraid to get any closer to the poor injured animal, but she knew she had to.

She dropped to her knees, gently smoothing the lank weeds away from the pitiful little shape. Trembling, she reached out her fingers and touched the soft fur, careful not to startle the creature. Its narrow chest was rising and falling rapidly, and its eyes were completely shut.

"Kitty . . . ?" Chloe whispered, her voice hoarse, her throat tight and burning. "I didn't mean it." A painful sob cut up through her throat like a sharp stone. Her face was wet with tears.

The injured cat's breathing became erratic. Chloe didn't know what to do. She knelt there, shivering and sickened — utterly horrified by what she had done.

Then the twisted little head turned and the eyes opened. The wounded animal looked up at her.

Chloe screamed.

She scrambled to her feet and ran helter-skelter back down the path. As she fought her way out through the broken gate, she heard at her back the fearful yowling and wailing of dozens of angry cats.

Chloe was terrified.

The gang was waiting for her, and Heather was grinning. "You clobbered it," she said. "That was so cool!"

"Get away from me!" Chloe shoved her hard. Heather lost balance. Her legs got tangled up in her bike and she fell over backward with a shout of anger and pain.

Chloe didn't even notice the others — they backed away from her as she ran across the road to where she had left her bike. She threw herself onto it and pedaled away from that dreadful nightmare as fast as she could — the tears stinging her cheeks as she sped homeward through the spiteful rain.

———

She managed to get indoors and up the stairs to the bathroom before she was sick. She kneeled with her head over the toilet bowl, her whole body racked with guilt. She heard her mother calling up the stairs.

Chloe washed her face and dried it with a towel, and answered back in as normal a voice as she could manage. "It's only me!"

"Are you OK?" her mother called up the stairs.

"Yes. I'm fine," Chloe replied weakly.

She was vaguely aware of some comments about making sure she put her bike away properly — and then silence. She sat on the bathroom floor with her cheek against the cold porcelain sink.

Chloe closed her eyes, but then she saw again in her mind the thing that had terrified her in the Cat Lady's front garden — the thing that had sent her running for her life from that horrible, horrible place.

She levered herself to her feet, flushed the toilet, and leaned over the sink. The sight of her own face in the mirror shocked her. Her skin was blotchy, smeared with the tracks of grimy tears and beaded with sweat. Her hair was sticking to her skin.

She turned on the faucets and watched as the clear water gradually filled the sink. Then she turned off the faucets and plunged her face into the water.

Lifting her head, Chloe looked again in the mirror. Now she was just pale — her fair hair like tangled ribbons on her cheeks and forehead. The haunted look was beginning to fade from her eyes.

Eyes.

Like the eyes that had . . .

No!

She wouldn't think about that.

A cold, hard determination was growing out of her misery. She was finished with Heather and the gang. Absolutely finished with all of them.

She shivered. She felt sweaty and cold, and her clothes were sticking unpleasantly to her.

Her legs felt stronger now.

She needed a shower.

A long, hot shower to try to wash away her feelings of wretchedness and grief. And then she had something important to do — something she should have done weeks ago.

Chloe pushed open the gate and wheeled her bike up the path. She rested it against the wall and stepped up onto the porch. She took a deep breath and pressed the bell.

In the long pause before anyone came to the door, she had plenty of time to imagine all the unpleasant things that might be said to her when the door opened.

There was the sound of a step behind the door. It swung half-open.

Her ex-best friend Tina stood on the threshold. She was shorter than Chloe, and not so thin, her dark hair cut into a neat bob that framed her round, friendly face. Not that her expression was at all friendly as she looked at Chloe. She stared at her in the way she might stare at something nasty she found on the sole of her shoe.

"Hello," Chloe said quietly.

"Hello." Tina's voice was cold and expressionless.

They hadn't spoken to each other for seven weeks and five days.

Chloe's mouth was dry. She attempted a smile. "How are you?" she asked.

Tina's voice was clipped and hard. "Fine. Thank you." She leaned against the door, staring into Chloe's face with a look of bored contempt in her eyes, as if waiting for Chloe to get this over with so she could go back to whatever she had been doing before the bell had rung.

Chloe swallowed. "I came to say I'm sorry about the T-shirt," she said.

"Isn't it a little late for that?" Tina said.

A voice called from somewhere in the back of the house. Tina's mom. "Who is it?"

"No one," Tina called back. "Chloe Forrester."

There was no response from her mother.

Chloe took a long, deep breath. "Look," she said. "I came to tell you I'll give you money for a new T-shirt. I've got some saved up — and you can have it all." Her heart was thumping. "I want us to be friends again." She swallowed hard. "But if you hate me — and if you don't ever want to speak to me again — then just say so and I'll go away right now and I'll keep out of your way forever."

There was a long pause.

Chloe wished the ground would open up and swallow her. This had been a bad idea. Tina would never forgive her.

After a moment, Tina took in a breath. "I might have been wrong about the T-shirt," she said. "Let's call it quits." She held the door wide. "Mom's made an apple pie. Want some?"

Chloe and Tina sat cross-legged on Tina's bed, eating apple pie topped with a dollop of whipped cream.

For a long time, Chloe was content to chat amiably with Tina, catching up on what had been going on over the past weeks, amazed at how easily they resumed their friendship again. It almost felt as if the rift had only lasted a day or two. And it was such a relief to Chloe that she could just be herself — that she didn't constantly have to act tough and cool to impress Heather and the gang.

But gradually, Chloe found herself talking about Heather's dare.

Tina shook her head. "You're such an idiot sometimes," she said as Chloe explained how she had given in to Heather's never-ending taunts and had agreed to throw that stone through the old lady's window.

Chloe looked at her. "I haven't told you the worst thing yet," she said in a subdued voice.

"You broke a window?"

Chloe shook her head. "I deliberately missed the window," she said. "But I hit a kitten." She shrank from the look of shock on her friend's face. "I didn't see it," Chloe blurted out, tears hot on her cheek. "It was lying behind a lot of tall weeds."

Tina's hands came up to cover her face. "Was it badly hurt?" she asked.

Chloe nodded, her throat tightening as the memory came flooding back.

"Did you call a veterinarian?" Tina asked.

Chloe shook her head. "It might have been too late."

"Chloe!" Tina exclaimed.

Chloe bit her lip. She couldn't look into Tina's face. As she spoke, she hardly recognized her own voice. "It was nearly dead," she breathed. "It was all twisted and helpless. But then . . . its head turned . . . and it . . . looked at me." She was trembling again now, reliving the horror of that impossible moment.

She stared into Tina's face. "Its eyes weren't *normal*," she whispered, hardly daring to put into words the terror that had been haunting her ever since.

"What do you mean?" Tina asked in a low murmur.

Chloe looked at her. "It didn't have a normal cat's eyes," she said. "Its eyes were — Tina, *it had human eyes!*"

That night, Chloe couldn't sleep. Her vision had long ago adjusted to the darkness, and she could easily make out the different shapes in her room. She wanted more than anything for this awful day to be over, but her brain wouldn't switch off. It was as if there were a lighthouse in her head, and its long, bright, sweeping beam was constantly turning to light up the darkest and most dreadful corners of her mind.

Tina had managed to convince her that she had imagined the spine-chilling thing about the cat's eyes. It couldn't have been real. It must have been a trick of the light or something. In any event, Tina had said, cats don't have eyes like people — they just don't!

And Chloe was more than happy to agree with her.

But still she couldn't sleep. In order not to seem weak in front of Heather and her stupid gang, she had done something that had harmed a kitten. And Heather had been impressed. "You clobbered it," she had said with a grin. Chloe shuddered.

She remembered something her mother had once told her. "A guilty conscience will never let you rest till you've made amends — until you've put things right."

That's why I can't sleep, Chloe thought. *I have to put things right.* But how do you put things right when you've potentially killed an innocent animal? What can you do? The answer came quite clearly into her head. *You can go to Mrs. Tibbalt's house and own up — and you can offer to help her in some way. You can make amends.*

Chloe decided that after school tomorrow, that was exactly what she was going to do.

Somehow, she would make amends.

Heather and the gang were waiting for her at the school gates the next morning.

"It's Chloe the Cat Killer," Heather said as Chloe approached. "That's what we're going to call you from now on. Like it, Killer?"

Chloe ignored her, but Heather wouldn't be ignored. She stepped into Chloe's path.

"Get out of my way," Chloe said flatly.

"Don't be like that," Heather said with a crooked smile. "We were worried about you — the way you ran off like that. But we were really impressed. I mean, smashing a window is one thing. But attacking one of the old woman's mangy little cats, that was totally impressive!"

"It made me sick, if you must know," Chloe said.

"What a shame," Heather said blandly. "Do you feel better now?"

Chloe stared coldly at her. "Not especially," she said.

Heather grinned, looking around at the others. "Tell her the good news," she said.

"We've voted," said Emma. "You're definitely a full-time member of the gang now."

Chloe stared at her in disbelief. "You think I still want to be in your pathetic gang?" she spat furiously.

"What's your problem, Killer?" asked Maggie.

"My problem is that you're a bunch of sickos — all of you!" Chloe glared at them. "I don't want anything to do with you. Just get out of my way!"

"Ooh — we'd better watch out," Hayley taunted her. "Killer's mad at us. Better make sure there are no rocks nearby!"

There was laughter.

Chloe pushed past them and stalked across the teachers' parking lot. Heather walked quickly after her. "Sorry you feel like that," she called, her voice filled with mockery. "But at least you've given us the idea for a really great new game." Chloe sped up, trying to get away from that sarcastic voice. "It's called 'Stone the Cats,'" Heather yelled after her. "We're going to try it out after school today if you're interested. You score points — one point for hitting a cat with a rock — five points if you wound it — and ten points if you stop it in its tracks." Her voice rose. "Hey, Killer — you've already got a ten-point lead on the rest of us. If you change your mind, we'll see you at the Cat Lady's place after school tonight." Laughter welled up in her voice. "And bring plenty of rocks!"

Chloe pushed down hard on the pedals as her bike sped along the road. School was done for the day. She had to get to Mrs. Tibbalt's house ahead of Heather and the gang — she had to warn the old lady what they were planning on doing. The cats had to be taken indoors — away from the cruel game that the gang intended to play.

She bounced her front wheel up over the curb and dismounted. Chloe noticed that the weeds had been cut down under the bay window and the ill-fated kitten was gone. She imagined the poor, lonely, frightened old lady coming out there the previous evening, picking up the limp body of the kitten, and shuffling into the house with it in her arms.

Putting her bike on the side of the path, she glanced up. There were no feline faces at the glass now. No accusing eyes.

Chloe's determination to warn the old lady about the gang was so strong that she forgot to be scared as she walked up the path.

She saw a dark shape streak out of the long grass and vanish around the side of the house. A cat. Another cat watched her suspiciously from the dappled shade of the shed roof. Their eyes met for a moment, then it slunk away into the shadows.

Chloe took a deep breath and stepped up to the

large front door with its peeling paint and rusty, unused mail slot. She searched for a bell, but there wasn't one. The iron doorknocker was in the shape of a leaping cat. She reached up to it. It was heavy and stiff, but she forced it up and brought it down.

Chloe waited, her heart beating hard and fast in her chest.

No one came to the door. She knocked again, and then looked down at her hands. The rust had stained her palms and fingers dark red.

Suddenly, she heard a yowling from within the house — the disturbed-sounding voices of several cats.

But still no one came to the door.

Chloe crouched, prying open the mail slot. The hallway was dark, with brown walls and a brown staircase at the far end.

"Mrs. Tibbalt?" she called through the slot. "Hello! Are you home? I need to talk to you!"

She stood up again, bringing the knocker down hard once more. There were grimy side panels of stained glass. Chloe rubbed them with her sleeve to try to clear away some of the dirt. She peered through, but she couldn't see much — and there was no sign of movement in the gloomy hallway.

She looked at her watch, her frustration and anxiety building. The old woman hardly ever left the house — she *had* to be in there, why wouldn't she come to the door? Chloe was becoming frantic — if Heather and the gang really did mean to come over here to throw stones at the cats, then they would only be a few minutes . . . they could arrive in the alley at any moment.

She ran to the bay windows and tried to clean the filthy glass with her hands, peeking in through the gray veil of the gauze curtains. She could see moving shapes in there — low on the ground. More cats. But was the old lady in there with them? Chloe rapped her knuckles on the glass.

Something flew at her face, startling her and making her stumble back — a large black cat, its eyes blazing, its red mouth wide open as it spat viciously at her. Long, unsheathed claws scraped against the window.

Was it the same cat she had first seen at the window the previous afternoon?

Had it recognized her?

Did it hate her for what she had done?

She ran to the side of the house. There was a side alley, but it was blocked by a tall black gate fastened with a padlock that had long ago rusted solid.

But Chloe couldn't give up now. She had to try to do something.

The wood around the padlock was rotten. She wrenched frantically at the rusty metal hasp. It came loose, and the padlock fell to the ground with a dull thud. She pushed the gate, and it swung open slowly on creaking hinges. She stepped through into the long, narrow side alley. At the far end, she could see a section of the overgrown back garden.

It was filled with cats.

Cats lying in pools of afternoon sunlight. Cats grooming themselves. Cats just sitting and staring. Cats play-fighting. Cats sharpening their claws. Cats on the prowl. A whole world of cats.

A moment later, every almond-shaped eye was staring uneasily at her.

Chloe swallowed hard. There was something unnerving about the way the cats were watching her. She began to walk down the alley. A few cats moved away out of sight around the back of the house. Others just watched her warily as she approached the garden.

A small, dark shape hissed and streaked away from her. A dark brown cat, sharp-faced and thin. It must have been lying unseen in the dark alley.

"Sorry, kitty," Chloe called. "I didn't mean to frighten you."

She came out into the garden. More cats streaked away from her, heading in a multicolored flood toward the open back door of the house. Those that didn't move watched her intently. Some hissed and arched their backs, tails up like spiking brushes, sharp teeth bared.

Chloe moved slowly, determined not to scare the animals. She edged along to the door.

"Mrs. Tibbalt?" she called. "Are you home?"

There was still no response.

She turned and looked into a small, dingy kitchen. A large part of the floor was cluttered with food and water bowls. There was a strong smell of cat food — but Chloe noticed right away that although the place was shabby and old and in need of a coat of fresh paint, it was nothing like the filthy hovel that Heather had described.

A couple of cats that had lingered in the kitchen sped away now through the open inner door. Braver cats scrutinized her from safe vantage points — on top of the fridge and on high shelves.

The door from the kitchen into the hallway stood half open. She reached for the handle, then gave a startled cry as the door opened on its own. A dark shape filled the doorway. Chloe stumbled backward, her foot caught on a cat bowl, and she slipped and fell, clattering among the food and water bowls as she sprawled on the linoleum.

"Good heavens!" came a kind but startled voice. "You gave me such a fright!"

It was Mrs. Tibbalt. She was carrying a cardboard box in her arms.

"I'm sorry," Chloe gasped. "I'm so sorry." She scrambled to her feet. "I knocked and called, but you didn't hear me, and I had to talk to you — so I came around the back. I didn't mean to scare you." She looked at the wreckage at her feet. "I'm so sorry — I've made a mess."

"I was in the basement," said the old lady. "Fetching food for my babies." She limped awkwardly into the room and put the box on the kitchen table. It was a box of canned cat food.

The scary old tales from the school playground slid into Chloe's mind — the big grinding machine. Now that she was face to face with Mrs. Tibbalt, the stories seemed absolutely ridiculous.

And I've been scared of her all this time because of them, she thought. *I am such an idiot!*

Staring at the box of cat food, she gave a burst of involuntary laughter, stifling it by bringing her hand up to cover her mouth. There was nothing here to be scared of.

The old lady looked at her. She was dressed in a blouse and a skirt. Without the odd kerchief and the bulky, threadbare coat, she looked almost normal. She limped back to the door and took hold of a cane that stood in the corner.

Mrs. Tibbalt leaned on her cane, her forehead creasing as she peered at Chloe.

"I know you," she said.

"I'm Chloe Forrester," Chloe said. She pointed through the back door and down the garden. "I live on the new side of town."

Mrs. Tibbalt nodded. "Aren't you one of the girls who stare over my fence?" Her eyes narrowed suspiciously. "You like to scare my babies. That's not very kind, you know."

Chloe swallowed and nodded. "Yes, I know. And I'm sorry. But please listen to me, Mrs. Tibbalt — the other girls — they're coming here right now. They're going to throw rocks at your cats. It's a horrible game they've invented. You have to get your cats indoors; otherwise they're going to get hurt."

The old lady looked sharply at her. "Now, why would anyone come up with a cruel game like that?" she said. Chloe had the unnerving feeling that Mrs. Tibbalt knew exactly what she had done the previous day.

Chloe felt remorse welling up in her. "I was here yesterday," she said slowly. "The other girls dared me to throw a rock at your window." Her voice trembled with shame. The woman watched her without speaking. "I missed the window — but I hit a kitten." She swallowed hard and looked into the old lady's eyes. "Did it survive?"

"She was called Sophie," Mrs. Tibbalt said. "She was six months old. I got her from a family who didn't want her. That's where most of my babies come from. I give them a home and look after them."

Tears stung Chloe's eyes as she realized the severity of her actions. "I know I've been saying I'm sorry ever since I arrived," she said in a choked voice. "But I really am more sorry than I can tell you."

"I believe you are," Mrs. Tibbalt said. "And now we'd better make sure your friends can't do any harm."

"They're not my friends," Chloe said firmly.

Mrs. Tibbalt smiled. She walked stiffly over to the back door and gave a long, low whistle. Moments later, cats began to streak in past her legs, ignoring Chloe as they rapidly filled the kitchen floor. More cats came running in from the rest of the house, and soon every flat surface in the room was filled with cats, rubbing against Mrs. Tibbalt's and Chloe's legs, purring and meowing.

Mrs. Tibbalt closed the back door. "There," she said. "All safe and sound." She looked at Chloe with a smile. "They think it's dinnertime — you can help me feed them, if you like. That way they'll start to forgive you for what you did. The can opener is in the drawer next to the stove."

Chloe returned the smile, liking the old lady a lot. "And will you forgive me, too?" she asked.

"Of course, I will," Mrs. Tibbalt said. "Cheer up, now — there are plenty of mouths to feed."

"Of course," Chloe said. She waded ankle deep through furry bodies.

For the next few hectic minutes, she helped Mrs. Tibbalt put out food for the cats. Soon, every bowl had a furry head or two in it, and the kitchen was filled with the sound of contented purring.

"Now it's time for *us* to have a little something," said Mrs. Tibbalt. "I usually make myself a nice cup of cocoa around this time." She smiled at Chloe. "Do you like cocoa?"

Chloe nodded.

"Me, too," Mrs. Tibbalt said.

Chloe watched as the cats ate and Mrs. Tibbalt made the cocoa in a small saucepan on the stove.

She poured out two steaming mugs. "There's nothing like cocoa on a cold afternoon," Mrs. Tibbalt said. "Let's go and sit."

She led Chloe along a dark corridor and into her

living room. It was decorated in a very old-fashioned way, with dark wallpaper and a sofa and armchairs covered in a faded floral pattern. The walls were dotted with pictures of cats. Porcelain cats stood on the mantelpiece, and photos and drawings of cats all in odd, old frames were arranged along the sideboard in a bizarre way.

Mrs. Tibbalt sat in an armchair, and Chloe sat in the corner of the huge sofa. Chloe felt comfortable and completely at ease with the friendly old lady. She sipped the frothy steaming cocoa. She looked at Mrs. Tibbalt. "This is delicious," she said.

Mrs. Tibbalt smiled. "It's my secret recipe," she said.

Chloe settled deeper into the corner of the soft sofa. "How many cats do you have?" she asked. "I've often wondered — but it's not easy to count cats."

"I have sixty-seven," Mrs. Tibbalt said, watching Chloe with bright, welcoming eyes over the rim of her cocoa mug. She frowned. "No, sixty-six, of course. I was forgetting poor little Sophie."

"I'd do anything for that not to have happened," Chloe said.

"What's done is done," the old lady said.

"I've been so stupid."

"It was an accident," Mrs. Tibbalt said gently. "You said yourself you didn't intend to hurt Sophie."

Chloe shook her head. "I don't mean that," she said. "I meant I've been stupid for being scared of you all this time." She laughed softly. "You're not scary at all."

"Well, thank you, Chloe," Mrs. Tibbalt said.

"I've always wanted a cat of my own," Chloe said. "But my dad is allergic to them." She looked at the old lady. "Would it be OK for me to come and visit you now and then? I'd love to help out with the cats."

"I think that's a wonderful idea," said Mrs. Tibbalt.

"I could come after school some days," Chloe said. She yawned. "Oh! Excuse me!" She smiled a dreamy smile, feeling warm and cozy and just a little bit drowsy.

"I'd like that," said Mrs. Tibbalt. "I don't get many visitors."

"I could visit lots," Chloe said. Her eyelids were beginning to feel strangely heavy. She blinked stupidly, fighting the drowsiness. "I'm so sleepy," she said. "Isn't that odd?"

Mrs. Tibbalt and the whole room were swimming in and out of focus. Chloe couldn't understand why she was suddenly so tired. Maybe it was because she had been so restless last night — or maybe it was because the sofa was so comfortable and the cocoa was so warm and sweet.

"I know you've forgiven me," Chloe said, her voice slurring, her limbs feeling heavy, her head starting to nod. "But do you know what I'd really like to do?"

"No, dear, tell me what you'd really like to do."

"I'd like to make amends," Chloe breathed. "I'd like to . . . make up for . . . for . . . everything . . ."

Mrs. Tibbalt's words came to her through a thick gray fog. "I'm sure we'll be able to come up with some way for you to fully repay your debt."

Chloe's chin drooped onto her chest. Her eyes fell closed. She was vaguely aware of the cocoa mug being refilled, even though it was still nearly full. She fought the overwhelming tiredness.

"I should . . . go . . . home . . . soon . . ." she murmured.

"Oh, not just yet, my poor sleepy girl. Drink up. You seem so nice, I might keep you."

With a supreme effort, Chloe lifted her head and forced her eyes open. Mrs. Tibbalt was leaning over her, and from the lined and wrinkled old lady's face, the bright yellow eyes of a cat were staring at her.

Chloe awoke. A cold draft was blowing over her face. She was curled up on the sofa. Mrs. Tibbalt was gone.

Chloe blinked, wondering what had happened and how much time had passed. Then she remembered feeling very, very tired. She must have dozed off. She smiled, still feeling sleepy and relaxed. She yawned widely and tried to get to her feet.

Her body didn't seem to want to obey her. She tried two or three times to stand up, but she kept falling onto all fours. Shaking her head to try to clear her thoughts, she crawled along the sofa and somehow got herself down onto the carpet.

The cold air was coming through the open door. She crawled dizzily into the hallway. The front door to the house was open. Chloe could see that it was getting dark out. Her mom would be wondering where she was. She had to get home.

Again, Chloe tried getting to her feet — again she fell back onto all fours.

She blundered toward the open doorway, bumping against the walls as she crawled slowly onward.

She came out onto the cold stone front step.

She looked out into the weed-filled garden and the out-of-control hawthorn hedges. She wondered where Mrs. Tibbalt had gone — and why the kind old lady had left her sleeping on the sofa.

But the main thought in her head was that she needed to get home.

She crawled down off the step. A movement in the corner of her eye caught her attention. Everything was strangely blurry, but very bright, and tinged with a curious greenish light so that moving shapes stood out very clearly from the fuzzy background.

The Cat Lady was wheeling a bike across to the rickety garden shed under the trees.

That's my bike, Chloe thought. She watched as Mrs. Tibbalt opened the shed door and pushed the bike inside. For the few brief moments that the door was open, Chloe caught a glimpse of several other bikes — and a pile of balls and toys, all heaped up on top of one another. Some looked as if they had been there for years. Then the door closed.

A chilling memory came back to her. A terrifying memory! The memory of the old woman's face looking down at her — staring at her with cat's eyes!

Chloe lurched down the front path, her head still spinning, her limbs only just obeying her as she made for the half-open front gate.

Somehow she got through without being seen.

Home. Get home, Chloe thought. *Home is safe.*

Soon she was in the alley and then at her own back gate. But she couldn't seem to reach up to lift the latch.

Perhaps I hurt my arm, she thought as she tried again. Focusing, she made a lunge for the latch, and to her amazement, she found herself balancing easily on the top of the gate. The kitchen window was a blaze of bright light — she could see her mother at the stove.

She jumped down lightly from the gate and ran up the path.

"Mom!" she called. "Mom, it's me! I can't get in. Help me." But her own voice sounded odd, and her mom didn't seem able to see her.

The door opened suddenly.

"Mom!" Chloe exclaimed, relieved.

Her mother looked down at her in surprise. "What are you doing here?" she said. "What do you want?"

"I want to come in," Chloe sobbed in frustration — again she couldn't make sense of her own words.

"I've got nothing for you," her mother said. "You can't come around here begging for food — if my husband saw you, he'd kick you over the back fence."

"Who are you talking to, Mrs. Forrester?" Chloe heard a familiar voice and looked over to the kitchen door. Tina was standing there.

"It's a cat," said Chloe's mother. "I heard it scratching at the door and meowing."

Chloe couldn't understand what was going on. Was this some kind of silly practical joke that Tina and her mother were playing on her?

Arms reached out for her, and she felt herself lifted into the air. Her mother's scent was very strong in her nose. Tina came over and stroked her head.

"Isn't it pretty?" Tina said. "Its fur is almost exactly the same color as Chloe's hair."

Chloe tried to speak, but the only sounds that came out were incoherent yowling.

"Good heavens — it's a noisy creature!" said Chloe's mother. "I'm sure it doesn't belong to anyone on our street. I think it must be one of Mrs. Tibbalt's strays." She smiled and scratched between Chloe's ears. "We should get it out of here before Chloe arrives home — otherwise she'll only want to keep it." She frowned. "Where is that girl? She should have been home by now."

"Mom, I'm here!" Chloe yowled. "I'm right here!"

"She told me she had something important to do after school," Tina said. "I'm sure she'll be back soon."

Mrs. Forrester smiled. "Well, I'm glad to see that the two of you are friends again," she said. "Tina, could you be a dear and take it to Mrs. Tibbalt's house for me and find out if it belongs to her?"

Chloe struggled and howled as Tina took her out of her mother's arms.

"You're right," Tina said, holding Chloe tightly. "It does talk a lot! And it wriggles like crazy. I'll take it right back."

Chloe gave up struggling. She was feeling light-headed from exhaustion and from the shock of what was happening to her. She hung limply in Tina's arms

46

as she was carried down the garden and out into the alley.

"Who's a pretty thing?" Tina crooned, stroking her head. "Wouldn't Chloe love to keep you? Yes, she would. Oh, yes, she would."

"I'm . . . Chloe . . ." Chloe said sadly.

"Aren't you chatty?" Tina said. "Are you hungry? Have you lost your mommy? Don't worry, I'm taking you home right now."

Chloe gave up trying to speak. She needed a few moments' rest so she could figure out how to explain everything to Tina.

Cradling Chloe carefully in one arm, Tina reached up and rapped the door with the knocker in the shape of a leaping cat. The door opened almost immediately.

"Hello there," Mrs. Tibbalt said to Tina.

"We found this cat — is it one of yours?" said Tina.

Mrs. Tibbalt smiled. "Yes, she is!" she said. "She's my little Sophie. I wondered where she'd gone." She reached out and took Chloe out of Tina's arms.

Just a few more seconds, Chloe thought, *then I'll be feeling better and I'll be able to explain to them who I am.*

"Thank you for bringing her back," Mrs. Tibbalt said. "It was very kind of you."

"No problem," Tina said. She turned and walked back down the path.

"You naughty runaway, Sophie," the Cat Lady said as she closed the door. "I can see I'm going to have to keep you locked up safe and sound indoors for a while — we can't have you running off all the time."

She carried Chloe to a door under the stairs. She opened the door and pushed Chloe into a dark room. The door closed and everything went black.

Chloe felt terrified and helpless. She could hear Mrs. Tibbalt walking away from the door — and she could hear the sounds of all the cats in the house: claws clicking on floorboards; contented purring; cats speaking and rubbing against Mrs. Tibbalt as she moved among them.

Her eyes quickly adjusted to the darkness. A flight of wooden steps led down to a cellar. Chloe ran down the steps, hoping desperately that she would be able to find a way out of here. The concrete floor was cold under her feet. She looked cautiously around, sniffing, her ears cocked forward, her whiskers quivering.

Something had been done to her — she had to accept that now. Something monstrous. Something unbelievable.

She ran distractedly around the basement, searching for a way of getting free — of getting back home. She was certain that if she could escape, she could find some means of letting her mother know what had happened. Then everything would be put right again. Mom would know what to do.

She spotted a high, narrow window. It had been covered by a sheet of plasterboard, but there was a chink of light in an upper corner where the board had begun to come away.

Chloe jumped for the window. She managed to keep her balance on the narrow sill as she clawed wildly at the plasterboard.

I have to get home. I have to find Mom! she thought frantically.

She could hear cats yowling and scratching at the cellar door — as if they somehow knew that she was trying to escape.

Her claws tore into the plasterboard. It came loose and fell away.

Desperation filled Chloe. She could see tall weeds — but they were beyond a wire mesh. She pushed hard against the mesh. It gave a little and a gap opened to one side — but it wasn't wide enough for her to squeeze through.

She heard Mrs. Tibbalt's footsteps approaching the cellar door. She heard the door open. She heard the sound of claws clattering on the stairs. The cats were coming to get her — she only had a few more moments to escape.

She fought madly against the wire mesh — ignoring the pain as it caught her fur and scratched her skin. She made a final frantic effort and burst free.

Panting and weak from the struggle, she found herself in Mrs. Tibbalt's backyard. Gasping with relief, she streaked down the yard toward the fence.

Heather was disappointed and annoyed. She stared over the fence, her pockets filled with rocks. There wasn't a single one of those mangy, flea-bag cats in the Cat Lady's yard. It looked as if their new game would have to wait for another time.

Suddenly, she saw a single, small cat come racing

down the garden from the house — straight toward the fence.

"I'll nail it!" she spat. She drew her hand back; a rock sat in her palm that was the size of a clenched fist. She snapped her arm forward and the rock flew.

"Yesss!" Heather gave a hiss of triumph. "That's a ten!"

WHO DARES WINS

"Haiii-yah!"

Mark Trent twisted the joystick and punched his fingers down on the control buttons of the videogame console. The samurai figure on the screen leaped and twirled in a blur of colored light. There was a slicing sound, a scream, and an electronic roar. The samurai came to rest. His final opponent, the Rogue Ronin Master, lay decapitated in a spreading pool of lurid vermilion blood. The screen exploded into a mass of dazzling fireworks, and the arcade rocked to the blare of triumphant, beat-heavy music.

Mark grinned around at his best friend, Calvin

Jenkins, and laughed as his score clicked up to twenty-seven — equaling Calvin's again.

"Cool!" said one of the small crowd of boys who had gathered around the two friends. He looked at Calvin. "Go on — keep playing," he said.

Mark stepped aside from the game and Calvin took his place.

He glanced around at the gathered faces. "What's the highest ever score?" he asked.

"Conner, a friend of ours, got thirty," one of the boys said.

Calvin lifted an eyebrow. "Easy," he said nonchalantly.

Mark smiled as he leaned against the side of the console.

He glanced over to a nearby game, where a girl he had never seen before was playing a game that he and Calvin didn't like much. She'd been at the game for some time and she seemed to be doing well — as far as Mark could make out, she was still on her first token.

He turned to watch as Calvin punched the START button and began to play. The screen ignited into noise and color as Calvin's samurai began to hack its way through the Ronin's army. Calvin always went in fast — as if he was trying to take the game by surprise. Punch — kick — slash! Quick and ferocious.

Mark preferred a slower, more measured approach. He liked to use strategy. To outthink his opponents.

Mark had lived two blocks away from Calvin for his entire life. They had been best friends and fierce rivals for as far back as he could remember. If Mark did something well, then Calvin had to try to do it better. And if Calvin succeeded in something, then, of course, it was only natural for Mark to do his utmost to beat him. That was just the way they were, whether it was sports or games or schoolwork. As far as Mark was concerned, their competitiveness didn't get in the way of them being best friends — it just gave their friendship an interesting edge.

Mark looked at his friend as he played the game, his short, stocky body hunched over the controls, his wild mop of dark hair hanging into his eyes. Calvin reminded him of a bull terrier — fearless and determined and always pushing forward. Mark wasn't quite so aggressive; he tended to think before he acted. He was taller than Calvin, lanky and thin with fine brown hair and hazel eyes.

More people were beginning to filter into the arcade, and outside the day promised to be bright and fine. It was two weeks into summer vacation. The weather was great and the new school year was too far away even to bother thinking about.

The arcade was on the beachfront. Through the open doors, across the road and beyond the railings, long piers rose above a rising tide of frothy white foam that sizzled on the pebbles like fizzy soda pop.

Mark watched attentively as Calvin's samurai hacked and chopped his way through the Ronin's palace. He had picked up three injuries — six would be fatal — and there were still plenty of opponents lining up in the corridors that led to the Ronin's inner sanctum.

"Watch out for the guy with the throwing stars," Mark warned.

"I see him," Calvin said, twisting and jerking the joystick. His samurai leaped and swerved, the long, curved sword slashing and hacking.

A moment later, there was a zapping sound as Calvin's warrior got hit in the chest with a star.

"You got another injury there," Mark said, grinning.

"I won't be the only one if you don't keep quiet!" Calvin growled, a look of absolute concentration on his face as he wrestled with the joystick.

"Just trying to be helpful," Mark said with a laugh. "Don't take it so seriously."

"Me take it seriously?" Calvin barked. "You're the one who always has to place first."

"No way," Mark said. "I'm just naturally good at things — you're the one who turns everything into a big deal."

"Huh!" Calvin snorted. "So why were you so annoyed when I got the same number of goals as you last season?"

"Because your seventh goal was a total fluke, that's why," Mark retorted. He laughed. "Be careful of that guy with the hook and chains."

"I'm on it!"

Mark watched in silent approval as Calvin's samurai cut down the last of the guards and headed for the inner sanctum of the castle.

Fifteen seconds later, there was a yell of approval from the crowd as Calvin dispatched the Ronin Master.

"Twenty-eight to twenty-seven," one of the kids called, looking at Mark. "Your turn."

The pressure was on Mark again. He was aware of Calvin watching him — waiting for him to make a mistake or to lose concentration.

But Mark wasn't about to let that happen. His samurai flipped and twirled and swung and sliced until there was no one left.

He smiled at Calvin. "I think that makes us even again, doesn't it?" he said, stepping aside.

"Not for long," Calvin said.

Mark glanced again toward the girl at the nearby machine. He guessed that she was about the same age as Calvin and him — thirteen. She was tall and quite skinny and dressed all in black — T-shirt, jeans, shoes, everything. She had cool, shoulder-length black hair with deep bangs that hung over her eyes.

She was playing Spidershadow. That was weird. Girls his age rarely came into the arcade and, when they did, they stuck together in giggling packs, cheering on the boys or stuffing quarters into the ancient Ms. Pacman machine in the corner. It was a lame game, a total waste of space. Mark was convinced they just liked it because it was pink. Not that he had anything against girls. In fact, he and Calvin had decided this year that maybe they weren't so bad after all. But he'd never met a girl who knew what to do with herself in an arcade. At least, until now.

It was weird enough that this girl had chosen to play Spidershadow, which was filled with plenty of shooting and explosions, all that stuff that usually made the girls squeal. But that wasn't the really strange part. The strange part was this: She was winning.

Spidershadow was one of the newest games in the arcade, and the toughest. A laser rifle was mounted on the front of the cabinet, but it wasn't a simple shooting game. There was an eight-way joystick and six command buttons as well as the rifle. The object of the game was to stalk a gang of special-forces soldiers "gone bad" through multitiered arenas and then take them out with shots from the rifle.

The problem was that the soldiers worked in two teams of three — and unless you were really quick in swapping from the joystick and buttons to the rifle, then one of them would shoot you before you had time to shoot all three of them. Mark and Calvin had given up on the game after one frustrating morning in which they were killed over and over again. It was an impossible game to win, they decided — not worth playing.

But the girl seemed to be playing it just fine. Mark watched as she maneuvered the joystick, her fingers dancing rapidly over the buttons.

Mark was intrigued. There was something that fascinated him about the way she just stood there — looking really cool and relaxed — while her long fingers pecked at the buttons. Then, with a sudden speed that startled him, she grabbed the rifle. Three shots rang out. The screen flashed and exploded as the three bodies lay dead.

She grabbed the joystick again and set off in search of the second trio of special-ops soldiers. Mark was impressed and intrigued. How had she done that?

There was something written in white on the front of the girl's T-shirt, but Mark could only make out the words *I'm up* and *What more.*

The speedy fingers pecked at the buttons again; the joystick wove and swung. For the second time, she snatched at the rifle. There were three quick shots as she swung the rifle around. *Crack-crack-crack.* Three more dead soldiers. The game was over.

Mark could hardly believe it. The girl had just walked in off the street and beaten that game in less than half an hour — a game that loads of other kids had spent all their pocket money on without winning once. She was way cool!

She stepped away from the game and turned toward them. She had the most amazing eyes that Mark had ever seen. They seemed to be silver. He had never seen anyone with silver eyes before. He couldn't stop staring at her.

She took a step toward the crowd of boys, folded her arms, and watched expressionlessly as Calvin played the game.

Now Mark could see what was written on her T-shirt.

I'm up and dressed.
What more do you want?

He grinned. That was good — he liked that. He wondered where she'd bought it.

Suddenly, she turned her head and those startling silver eyes looked straight at Mark. A smile crept up one side of her face.

It was a strange smile — amused and slightly mocking, very cool and self-possessed.

Mark looked quickly away, realizing that he had been staring at her. That wasn't like him at all. He liked girls and he got along with them at school and so on — but he'd never met a girl that he couldn't stop staring at. It was weird.

"Are you playing, or what?"

A finger poked him in the arm. He stared at Calvin with his mouth half open. He felt like he'd just been dragged up out of deep black water.

"What?"

"Do you want to try and get even with me — or are you giving up?" Calvin asked, grinning. Mark looked around. While he'd been distracted by the girl, Calvin had brought his score up to twenty-nine. "You can admit defeat right now, if you like," Calvin said. "I'll only beat you anyway."

"In your dreams," Mark said, turning to the machine.

But his concentration was broken. Even as Mark banged his hand down on the START button, he glanced across to where the girl had been standing.

She was gone.

He frowned, looking around the bustling arcade, hoping to catch sight of her again. But there were too many people in there now — too much going on.

The machine let out a blast of music. Mark stared at the screen. His samurai warrior was lying on the courtyard floor with its head cut off.

"Pathetic!" Calvin crowed, elbowing Mark out of the way and taking the controls. "You've got to concentrate. What were you thinking?"

Mark stepped aside. He felt slightly dazed and somewhat idiotic.

He stared at the small crowd, trying to find her. But she was gone. He hardly even noticed when Calvin won the next game.

Mark and Calvin came out of the crowded arcade and onto the street. Calvin had ended up beating him thirty-one to twenty-nine. The sidewalks were thick with vacationers. It was time to get out of here.

"Well, you certainly crashed and burned in there," Calvin said. "What happened?"

Mark shrugged. "I got bored," he said.

"Yeah — right!" Calvin chuckled. He sucked in the sea air. "So? What's the plan?"

"I don't know," Mark said blankly. "What's the plan?" He was staring up and down the beachfront road.

Calvin looked at him. "What's wrong with you?"

"Nothing." Mark frowned. "There was a girl," he said. "She was playing Spidershadow."

Calvin laughed. "Good luck to her," he said. "That game's impossible. Especially for a girl."

"She won," Mark said.

Calvin stared at him. "No way."

Mark nodded. "She did. I couldn't believe it, either."

"It was a fluke," Calvin said dismissively. "No girl could beat that game. You and *I* could barely get past level one!"

"I don't think it was a fluke," Mark said. "You have to beat two special-forces teams to win the game. One might be a fluke, but she got both. I was watching her. She was amazing."

Calvin's eyes narrowed. "What kind of amazing?" he asked.

It was at that moment — just when Mark had given up any hope of finding her — that he saw the girl over Calvin's shoulder. She was sitting on the low brick wall that ran alongside the arcade. The wall fronted a restaurant with an outdoor-seating area that was filled with noisy people.

"There she is," he said under his breath, nodding toward the girl. "Don't stare at her," he hissed — but too late. Calvin had already turned around.

The girl was gazing out toward the sea, listening to headphones.

Calvin walked straight up to her, Mark trailing awkwardly in his wake.

"What are you listening to?" Calvin asked.

The girl stared at him. "What?"

Calvin pointed to her headphones. "What music?"

The girl slid the headphones down around her neck. "Nothing you'll have heard of," she said. "Seagulls Screaming Kiss Her Kiss Her. They're Japanese. Completely awesome."

"My pal here says you beat Spidershadow," Calvin said.

Mark gave her a weak smile — feeling extremely embarrassed now that Calvin had made it so obvious that he had been watching her.

The girl leaned forward on the wall, her legs swinging. "That's right," she said.

"Have you played it before?" Calvin asked.

She shook her head, her sleek black hair moving like water on either side of her face. "It wasn't difficult. It's just a machine — you can always figure out what machines are going to do."

Calvin's eyes widened. "You know about machines? I thought girls were only into their hair and makeup and garbage like that."

The girl rolled her eyes at him and hopped off the wall as if to leave. "Sorry to disappoint you," she said.

"No, wait!" Mark yelped. She turned to look at him, and he blushed. "My friend didn't mean anything," Mark protested. "He just meant that we've never seen a girl so good at playing games. We think it's pretty cool."

Calvin grinned. "Very cool," he agreed. "I'm impressed.

My name's Calvin." He pointed over his shoulder. "This is Mark."

"I'm Chrissie," the girl replied.

"Are you here on vacation?" Calvin asked.

"Not really," she said vaguely.

Mark felt himself turning red. Chrissie was so cool, and Calvin was sounding like the biggest geek ever.

"I like the T-shirt," he said, desperate to get into the conversation. "Where did you get it?"

She looked down at herself. "A store," she said. "It isn't around here. It sells loads of cool stuff."

"So, you're a videogame freak, like us?" Calvin asked. Mark cringed. He wished Calvin would just *give it up*!

"Not really," Chrissie said. "They're a little boring. Like that one in there — that Spidershadow thing. I mean, it's OK for a while, but once you've played it, it's like — been there, done that — what's new?"

"The more you play, the better you get," Calvin said. He nodded toward the arcade. "I just beat the all-time record on Rogue Ronin. I got thirty-one — the previous record was thirty."

Mark winced — Chrissie didn't seem like she'd be impressed by that kind of thing.

"Good for you," Chrissie said in a slightly mocking tone.

Calvin frowned at her, obviously not sure what to make of her.

"So, how come you're so good at Spidershadow?" Mark asked.

She smiled. "Want to know the trick?" she asked. "You keep your fingers pressed down on the LOCATE and HIDE buttons until you fire the first shot. That way they can't get behind you."

"How did you know that?" Calvin asked.

"I figured it out," Chrissie said. She stood up quite suddenly. "Where's good to eat around here?" she asked. "I'm starved."

"There are burger joints and pizza places along the water," Mark said before Calvin had the chance to say something dumb. "But we usually go to a place down the block — it doesn't get so crowded there."

"Sounds good," Chrissie said. "Where is it?"

"We can show you," Mark said. "It's not far."

He felt self-conscious when she spoke to him, but there was something about her that he liked — and he wanted to know more about her.

The retro-style diner had a high, narrow counter that ran the length of the front window. The place was a lot busier than Mark had expected, and it was a while before they were able to find three stools together and continue their conversation.

They sat in a row: Calvin, Chrissie in the middle, and Mark in the corner, perched on tall stools while they ate.

"So," Calvin asked her. "Are you here on vacation?"

Chrissie shook her head, chewing and swallowing. "I'm here with my dad. He's working on a big building site on Lincoln Avenue."

"I know where you mean," Mark said, nodding. "It's in the main part of town."

"What does your dad do?" Mark asked.

Chrissie picked up a french fry and dipped it in a big pool of ketchup that she had poured onto her plate. "He's a builder," she said.

"So, are you living in town?" Mark asked. He hoped she would say yes.

"We're staying in a house up the street," Chrissie said. "It's a bit of a dump and it's full of the craziest people." She grinned. "There's this guy who lives in the basement. I've spoken to him a few times. He's really into reptiles, you know? He has snakes and lizards and stuff like that. He showed me them the other day: He keeps them in big fish tanks down there and he feeds them live animals — mice, insects, and worms."

Mark shuddered. "I don't like snakes," he said.

Chrissie bit the tip off her fry. "Oh, I don't mind snakes," she said. "They're kind of cute."

"So — if you're not doing anything, you could hang out with us, if you like," Calvin said. Mark felt a twinge of annoyance — he'd been about to say the same thing.

Chrissie looked at him. She wrinkled her nose. "Playing videogames?" she said dubiously.

"Scared we'll beat you?" Calvin asked with a grin. "I knew Spidershadow was just a fluke. No girl could be *that* good at games."

Mark felt his stomach clench. This was it: She was going to get offended again and walk out on them. *Great job, Calvin,* he thought in disgust. *Just great.*

But the girl just gave him a cryptic half-smile.

"Actually, girls are better at games than boys. It's a scientific fact."

"Yeah, right!" Calvin snorted. "In your dreams."

"I think it probably just depends on the person,"' Mark said, trying to play peacemaker between the new girl and his best friend. But even though he knew better than to say it out loud, he agreed with Calvin.

"If you're so good, then why are you afraid to play us?" Calvin challenged.

Chrissie smiled at him. Not a mocking half-smile this time, but a wide, dazzling smile that made Mark feel like the sun had suddenly burst out on a cloudy day.

"Oh, I'd be happy to play a game with you — and show you what girls can *really* do," she said. "Just not one of those lame videogames." She drowned another fry in the ketchup. "They're for dorks!"

"So, what kind of games do you like, then?" Mark persisted, recovering a little from the effects of the smile.

"Oh, just one game." Chrissie shook her head. "It wouldn't be your kind of thing," she said.

"Try us," Calvin said.

"There's no point," Chrissie said. "Even if I told you about it, you wouldn't be interested. You'd freak out."

"You mean it's dangerous?" Mark asked.

Chrissie tilted her head. "No," she said slowly. She smiled again, pointing to her head. "Only in here."

Mark couldn't make out what she meant.

Calvin shook his head. "She's making it up," he said to Mark. "She's just getting us riled up."

"It's called 'Who Dares Wins,'" Chrissie said. Her piercing silver eyes fixed on Calvin's face. "What are you most frightened of?" she asked.

Calvin pursed his lips thoughtfully. "Being kissed by my aunt," he said with a grin. "It's disgusting."

Mark laughed out loud. He'd met Calvin's aunt — he knew exactly what he meant.

But Chrissie just rolled her eyes. "I should have known better," she said wearily. "Boys are so immature." She turned toward the window. "Forget about it," she said.

"No," Mark said, eager for her to continue. "Tell us about the game — what are the rules? What do you have to do?"

"You have to face up to things that scare you," Chrissie said. "I heard about it from a guy I met when me and Dad were living in the city last year."

"What kind of things?" Mark asked.

"Different things for different people," Chrissie said. "For instance — I really hate having birds flying near my face. It just creeps me out for some reason. Like, they're going to peck my eyes out or something." She shivered. "So, I had to be locked in a room with a pet canary loose in it." She smiled. "It may not sound all that bad, but I was totally freaked by it," she said. "But I did it — I beat the game." She looked at Calvin again. "So, apart from being slobbered over by your aunt — what else don't you like?"

"I don't know," Calvin said. "There's nothing much."

"Oh, right," Mark said with a grin. "What about spiders?"

Calvin made a face. "OK, I'm not too crazy about spiders — but I'm not scared to death of them." He thrust a finger in Mark's face. "And what about you and canned tomatoes!"

Chrissie laughed. "Canned tomatoes?" she said. "You're kidding."

Mark shuddered. "I know it's a weird thing to have a problem with," he said, "but they just give me the creeps — especially those whole plum tomatoes. They look totally disgusting — like animal hearts all covered in blood."

"That's the craziest thing I've ever heard," Chrissie said. "What kind of person has a tomato phobia?"

"He knows that," Calvin said. "But it's like me and spiders. There's nothing you can do about it."

"There is if you play Who Dares Wins," Chrissie said. "That's the whole point of the game — to confront the things that scare you and beat them." She pointed at Mark. "You'd have to eat a plum tomato right out of a can." She turned to Calvin. "And you'd have to cope with having a spider crawl over you."

Mark's initial reaction was to tell her to forget it — he hated tomatoes that much. And he could see from the expression on Calvin's face that he didn't like the sound of the spider, either. He looked at her — trying to decide what to do. Play the game or wimp out?

"And what about you?" he asked her. "What would you have to do?"

"I've already beaten the game," Chrissie said. "So, I'll be Game Master. I'll set the rules and make sure you play the game the right way. And because you'll be competing against each other, we'll have to set up a forfeit system just to make it more interesting. Like, if either of you gives up, then they have to give something to the other one."

Mark looked at Calvin. "Are you up for it?" he asked.

"Why not? If a girl can beat the game, I'm sure *I* can." He shot a quick look at Chrissie. "No offense."

"None taken." Chrissie turned to Mark. "How about you?"

Something about the game still sounded a little strange to Mark, but he wasn't about to back down in front of Chrissie, especially now that Calvin had already said yes. "I'm in. What should we play for?"

A slow grin spread up the side of Calvin's face. "If you lose, I get your new Nike sneakers."

"And if you lose, I get your football jersey," Mark said, his eyes gleaming.

"So, when do we start?" Calvin asked. "And who goes first?"

"We can start right now," Chrissie said. She put her hand in her pocket and pulled out a coin. "Mark calls," she said, flipping the coin and slapping her hand down over it as it landed in her palm.

Mark drew a deep breath. "Heads," he called.

Chrissie lifted her hand.

It was tails.

"Plum tomatoes, here we come," Calvin said with a chuckle. He grinned at Mark. "You are *so* going to lose those sneakers!"

They were in the kitchen at Mark's house. No one was home; both his parents were at work and wouldn't be back for several hours.

Mark looked at Chrissie. She was sitting up on the counter, swinging her legs. He was sitting at the table with an empty plate and a knife and fork in front of him. Calvin was standing opposite him at the table, slowly twisting a can opener to lift the lid of a can of whole plum tomatoes that they had just bought.

Calvin tipped the can over the plate and the bulging soft red lumps of tomato came blubbering out in a splatter of thick, gory juice. Mark stared at the horrible mess on the plate. The tomatoes looked so revolting, lying there in a pool of red liquid, soft and flabby and skinned raw.

Calvin grinned at him. "You can give up now, if you want," he said. "Yuck," he said. "Hearts in their own blood. I think one of them is still throbbing away in there!"

Mark gave him a revolted look and shook his head. "You're not going to scare me."

Calvin laughed. "OK," he said. "No more tricks."

Mark stared hard at the plate in front of him. He couldn't ignore his disgust.

"Go for it," Calvin said. "I'd hate to take those sneakers away from you." He leaned forward, urging Mark on. "Come on — they're just tomatoes."

Mark picked up the knife and fork. "Do I have to eat all of them?" he asked in a small voice.

"Yes!" Chrissie said. "Chew 'em up, Mark."

He glanced at her; she seemed to be getting a real kick out of this.

Calvin frowned at her. "No," he said. "He just has to eat one."

Chrissie shrugged. "Fine," she said. "But he has to eat it with his fingers."

Mark had hoped that cutting the tomatoes into small pieces with the knife and fork might make it easier. The thought of having to pick one up in his hands and bite into it made the whole ordeal that much worse.

He put the knife and fork down and stared at the plate.

"You can do it," Calvin said.

Mark took a deep breath. He cleared his mind; thinking about it was only going to make it harder. He grabbed one of the tomatoes off the plate; he could hardly keep hold of it as it slipped through his fingers, dripping thick juice. He closed his eyes and opened his mouth.

He crammed in the nauseating fat mess. He leaned back, eyes closed, bringing his teeth down on the plump flesh. His hands were gripping the table edge. He chewed, feeling the soft tissue turn to disgusting mush in his mouth.

He swallowed three or four times.

The tomato was gone.

He opened his eyes and let out a gasp of laughter.

"Way to go, Mark!" Calvin shouted.

Mark took a long, deep breath. "That was the worst thing I have ever tasted," he said. His stomach heaved.

He scrambled to his feet. "I'm going to throw up!" he gasped. He ran to the sink.

"You won't be sick," Chrissie said. "Just drink some water. You'll be fine."

Mark hung over the sink.

No — he wasn't going to be sick. He refused to throw up in front of a girl. Especially a girl as cool and fascinating as Chrissie. He didn't want her to think he was a wimp. Mark poured himself a tall glass of water and drank it all at once.

He turned from the sink, looking at Calvin. He grinned. "Still think you're going to get my sneakers?" he said. "Now let's see how you manage with the spiders. There are some nice fat juicy ones down behind the shed in the garden."

Calvin gave him a laid-back look. "No problem," he said. "You can put half a dozen of them on me, if you like."

"No," Chrissie said, jumping down off the counter. "Just the one — but you have to eat it."

Mark laughed, assuming that Chrissie was teasing Calvin. But the expression on her face didn't suggest that she was joking.

Calvin was staring at her — he had turned pale.

"You can't make him *eat* a spider," Mark said.

"I'm Game Master," Chrissie said. "I decide the rules." She looked at Mark. "You had to eat a tomato — something that creeps you out. Calvin has to eat a spider — something that creeps him out. What's the problem?" Her eyes were bright and sharp. "Or we could forget the whole thing." She shrugged, a slightly scornful look coming over her face. "It's up to you."

"This is a stupid game," Calvin said.

"That's what boys always say when things get too tough for them." Chrissie said. Then her voice became soft and persuasive. "Oh, come on, Calvin. Don't give up. Mark beat the game. If you don't confront your fear of spiders, Mark will get your jersey — plus you'll feel pathetic. Do you want that to happen?"

Mark looked at his friend, trying to think of some way of persuading him to play the game. He'd eaten one of those revolting tomatoes; he at least wanted Calvin to *try* eating a spider before he gave up.

"You don't have to eat one of those big garden spiders," he said to Calvin. "How about one of those leggy ones with the tiny bodies that hang upside down in my dad's shed? And you could fold it up in a slice of bread — you wouldn't even notice it then." He looked at Chrissie. "That would be OK, wouldn't it?"

Chrissie smiled. "I'd prefer a big fat juicy one that pops in his mouth when he bites down on it," she said with slow relish. "But I suppose a spider is a spider." She shrugged. "OK. I rule that he passes the test so long as he eats a spider sandwich."

Mark looked at Calvin. "Are you up for it?"

Calvin nodded, his face still grayish, but his expression determined.

Mark took a slice of bread from the bread box. He unlocked the back door and led them down to the garden shed. He undid the padlock and stepped into the shed, feeling a momentary twinge of anxiety. He really wasn't good with small rooms and enclosed spaces.

It only took Mark a few moments to locate one of the spindly-legged spiders that were attached to the underside of the shed roof.

Calvin and Chrissie stood at the door as Mark raised the slice of bread up under the spider. He flipped it with his finger. The startled spider gave a spasmodic flurry of legs as it fell. Mark quickly folded the slice of bread over it.

He came out of the shed and handed the sandwich to Calvin.

"It's a bit rough on the spider," Mark said. "One minute you're minding your own business — the next you're someone's lunch."

"If Calvin eats it quickly, it won't even know what's happening to it," Chrissie said. "Besides — there are loads of things that eat spiders."

"But people don't," Calvin said in a dry-throated whisper. For a few long moments, he stood there staring at the folded slice of bread.

"If you pass this test, you get a reward," Chrissie said.

Calvin looked at her. "What?"

She smiled that wide, sweet, sunshine smile of hers. "You get to spend more time with me."

Mark felt a twinge of jealousy as he saw Chrissie smiling at Calvin. But a moment later it had passed, overshadowed by the thought of Calvin having to eat that spider.

Calvin laughed. Then he lifted the sandwich to his mouth. He hesitated for a split second before cramming the whole folded slice into his mouth. Mark could hardly watch as Calvin chewed up the bread.

"Swallow it — swallow it all up!" Chrissie crowed.

Calvin swallowed. He looked at Mark with a triumphant grin on his face. "I didn't taste a thing," he said. He laughed, pretending to wipe sweat off his forehead. "That wasn't so bad."

Chrissie frowned. "I made it too easy for you," she said. "Now that I think about it — I'm not sure it counts. I think you should eat one without any bread."

"No way!" Calvin said. "I did what you told me to do. You can't go changing the rules afterward."

"I'm Game Master," Chrissie said. "I make the rules."

"He ate the spider," Mark added. "That means he beat the game."

Chrissie looked from one to the other. "This is lame," she said. "Those things were pathetic. They weren't scary at all — not really scary. You don't have a clue about how to really play the game." She turned, arms folded, and marched out of the yard.

Mark and Calvin looked at each other in complete surprise.

"Hey! Come back!" Calvin called. "What's the problem?"

Chrissie turned at the garden gate. "No problem," she called back. "I've got things to do."

"Do you want to meet up somewhere later?" Mark called.

"Tell you what," she said. "If you can come up with some better fears that you feel like confronting, we'll play another round of the game. I'll be out near the arcade tomorrow morning about ten o'clock. If not — forget it."

And then she was gone.

Mark heard his front door slam.

"That is one seriously screwy girl," Calvin said. He looked at Mark. "Can you believe the way she blew up like that?"

But Mark was just thinking of her smile and of her wide silver eyes — and wondering what kind of thing he'd have to come up with in order to keep her interested in hanging out with him.

It was later that same afternoon. Mark and Calvin were sitting on the floor in Mark's room, playing ZOMBEEZ. It was a game that Mark had only bought the previous week, and they were both still getting used to it. It was set in the thirtieth century, and they were two police officers sent on a mission to an old cemetery to find and destroy the hidden spaceship of invading aliens who were busy reanimating the corpses of dead Earth people to create an army intended to take over the planet.

Neither Mark nor Calvin had yet managed to get anywhere near the heart of the spaceship before their health panels went critical and the game spat them out.

"Awesome graphics!" Calvin said as his character rounded a corner and came into a massive docking chamber filled with dart-shaped fighting ships. He walked across the floor, looking very small in the vastness of the silent room. Nothing moved.

"It's got to be a trap," Mark said.

"There's nothing in here," Calvin said, frowning as he concentrated on the screen.

"There's a strange pattern on the floor," Mark said.

"Wait — what's that —" Calvin began.

The screen erupted into white flames. His character gave a loud death-scream as his health panel dropped to zero.

The screen flashed: GAME OVER.

"We're never going to get into the control room at this rate," Calvin said. "Are there any hints in the booklet?"

Mark shook his head. "Maybe we can find something online?" He looked at Calvin. "I bet Chrissie could figure it out."

"I still say she can't be *that* good at videogames," Calvin said. "Besides, she'd just tell us what losers we are for playing it in the first place."

There was a short silence.

"She's kind of strange, isn't she?" Mark said.

"She's a nut job," Calvin said. "Did you see the way she lost her temper?"

"Well, yes, but . . ."

Calvin looked sharply at him. "But what?"

"I like her," Mark said. He gave a weak grin and shrugged his shoulders. "I don't know why — I just do. She's different."

"She's different, all right," Calvin said.

"Don't you like her?" Mark asked.

"I don't know," Calvin said. "Maybe."

Mark stood up. He stretched and walked over to the window. He looked down into the garden — seeing her face in his mind, remembering that smile.

He looked at Calvin over his shoulder. "If we were going to play that game of hers again, what could we come up with that we're scared of?"

"I'd tell her you're freaked by snakes for a start," Calvin said. "Or that you're scared of being trapped in small places."

Calvin was right. Mark hated snakes — and he was so claustrophobic that he hardly ever used an elevator. He only had to be in an enclosed space for a couple of minutes before he felt like he couldn't breathe, as if the walls were closing in on him, trying to suffocate and crush him.

"And I'd tell her how you feel about being in the woods," Mark retorted. "And your thing about heights."

"She probably wouldn't think they were interesting enough for her stupid game," Calvin said.

Mark turned. "So — are we going to meet up with her tomorrow?"

"I don't care, either way," Calvin replied nonchalantly.

"Neither do I." Mark looked sideways at his friend. "But we might as well go down there. What do you say?"

"Sure."

Mark smiled, relieved that the decision had been made. He couldn't figure Chrissie out — but he definitely wanted to see her again. He tried to make his voice sound as casual as possible. "Do you think she's OK-looking?"

"Yes," Calvin said after a short pause.

They caught each other's eyes for a moment, then looked away.

Mark lay awake for some time that night, thinking about Chrissie and picturing her in his head. And she was the first thing to pop into his mind the next morning when he woke up.

He came down into the kitchen. His dad was already

gone, but his mother was still at the breakfast table, reading the local newspaper as she drank from a mug of coffee and listened to the radio.

"Morning," Mark said, yawning as he opened the fridge. He scooped out a carton of orange juice and swigged from it.

"Use a glass," his mother said. "Do you want me to make you some breakfast?"

"No, I'll just have toast," he said, shuffling off to the cabinet, still yawning.

"Got any plans for today?" his mother asked. "Have you started your summer reading for school? I know you — if I don't keep reminding you, you'll leave it till the last minute."

Mark put bread in the toaster and hunted for the jam. "I'm about to start," he said. "I've got most of the books I need."

"Well, make sure that you read them," she said. She turned, leaning her arm on the back of the chair. "Do you remember those three kids who fell off the cliff a couple of weeks ago?"

Mark nodded. It had been big news for a few days. Three teenagers had disappeared near the cliffs that rose up to the east of town. Two of them had been severely injured, but the other was still missing. The Coast Guard thought she had been swept out to sea.

"There's an article in here today, saying that people should keep off the cliffs till the town puts up some safety fences," his mother continued.

"Even if the town puts up fences, some idiot or another will climb over it just to prove a point," Mark said.

"You don't ever go up there, do you?" his mother asked, her face serious.

Mark let out a dramatic sigh. "I'm not an idiot, Mom."

"I know that. All the same . . ."

"If you remember, Calvin is freaked out by heights," Mark said. "We never go up on the cliffs."

"Well, that's good." His mother carried her breakfast dishes over to the sink. "So?" she said. "What do you have planned today?"

Mark gave her a sideways look. "Me and Calvin met a girl in the arcade yesterday," he said. "We might meet up with her again."

"Is she nice?"

He felt a silly smile stretching across his face. He

quickly got it under control, but not before she spotted it.

"She's OK," he said nonchalantly. His mother grinned at him. "What?" he said defensively.

"Oh, nothing," she said. She moved in on him, taking his face between her hands before he had the chance to escape. "Beware of strange girls," she said. "Girls can be dangerous. Does Calvin like her, too?"

"I don't know," Mark said, trying not to laugh at the idea that girls could be dangerous. "I haven't asked him. Don't you have a train to catch?"

His mother glanced at the wall clock. "Yes, I do." She lifted her shoulder bag off the back of a chair. At the kitchen door, she looked back at him.

"Remember what I told you about girls you don't know," she said. "And remember what I said about those cliffs."

"'Bye, Mom," Mark said. Mothers could be so clueless sometimes. Chrissie was a lot of things — but dangerous wasn't one of them.

A few minutes later, he was sitting at the table eating toast and jam and staring at the wall clock. It was only half past eight.

They had arranged for Mark to pick up Calvin at home at ten o'clock and for them to go down together to meet up with Chrissie — but that was still an hour and a half away.

It seemed like a very long time.

Mark got to Calvin's house at half past nine. His older sister answered the door, still wrapped in a bathrobe and looking bleary. After going up and checking Calvin's room, she came back down and told Mark that Calvin had already gone out.

That was weird. Mark always picked up Calvin on the way down to the beachfront.

Then a thought hit him. An annoying thought. Had Calvin gone to meet Chrissie without him?

He walked quickly down toward the sea. He saw Calvin and Chrissie immediately. They were sitting close together on the railings that overlooked the beach.

Mark dodged through the traffic to reach them. He leaned on the rail at Chrissie's elbow. "Hi, there," he said.

The two heads turned.

"Hello," Chrissie said.

Calvin gave Mark a slightly guilty look.

"I went to your house," Mark said. "I thought we'd arranged to meet there."

"I was up early, so I thought I might as well come down here," Calvin said. "I knew you'd find us."

Chrissie swung her long legs over the rail and jumped down onto the pavement. She had a different slogan on her T-shirt today:

I'll stop wearing black
when they invent a darker color.

"I thought we were supposed to meet at ten," Mark said.

Chrissie looked at him with a half-grin. "What are you — Captain Stopwatch or something?"

"No," Mark said, suddenly feeling a bit small and petty. But on the other hand, Calvin was the one who had said he thought Chrissie was a nut job — and here he was meeting up with her on his own.

"So," Chrissie said to him. "You're claustrophobic, huh?"

"A little," Mark said. He swung his legs over the railings and hitched himself up so he was sitting next to her. "But I'm not freaked by little spaces as bad as Calvin is freaked by heights."

Chrissie looked at Calvin. "You never mentioned that," she said.

"And has he told you that he has this thing about forests?" Mark made a wide gesture with one arm, to indicate the general direction of the patch of woodlands behind the town.

Calvin looked at Chrissie. "When I was a little kid — five or six years old — I wandered off on my own and got lost in the woods. It got dark and I freaked myself out, that's all. I couldn't sleep for a few days. It was no big deal."

"He still won't go in there," Mark said, enjoying his friend's discomfort.

Chrissie looked at Calvin. "Is that true?"

"I don't like the place," Calvin said, folding his arms defensively over his chest. "But I'm not *scared* of it."

Mark grinned at Chrissie. "It sounds like a phobia to me," he said. "If we're going to continue playing the game, then I think Calvin's challenge has to be to go into the woods at night — and stay there on his own for an hour."

"Blindfolded, and with his hands tied," Chrissie added with sudden enthusiasm. "Yeah — that would be awesome!" She looked at Calvin. "You really should do it. Think of how great you'll feel if you conquer your fear."

"It's not dark until late at this time of year," Calvin said. "My folks won't let me be out in the woods at night."

Chrissie looked at him. "Ever heard of lying?" she said sarcastically. "You tell your parents that you're over at Mark's house and he tells his parents he's at your house — and both of you come with me to the woods."

"And what do we do after the game?" Mark asked. "Where do we sleep?"

"Oh, come on," Chrissie said, her eyes bright and eager. "I'm sure you can come up with *something*, no?"

Mark looked at Calvin. "We could easily get back into my house without anyone hearing," he said. "So long as we keep quiet till my folks have left for work, they'll never suspect anything."

Calvin nodded. "I suppose so," he said.

"There you go," Chrissie said, smiling. "Easy!" She looked at Mark. "And I know exactly what to do for your test." She leaned forward and whispered something in Calvin's ear. Mark felt a stab of jealousy as a wide grin spread over Calvin's face.

"Can you get one?" he asked. Chrissie nodded.

"As well as hating confined spaces, Calvin tells me you're scared of snakes," Chrissie said. "So while Calvin is dealing with his fear of the woods, I think I should be introducing you to a nice, slimy, slithery snake."

Mark looked at her, trying hard to cover up how much the idea scared him.

"Cool," he said, managing to give her a casual grin. "Just so long as I don't have to eat it."

"No," Chrissie said. "You won't have to eat it." She smiled. "You'll just have to *wear* it."

"What's the plan for today?" Calvin asked. "We can't play the game till tonight."

"I have to go right now," Chrissie said. "I'll catch up with you guys later."

"I thought we were going to hang out," Mark said.

"We are — *tonight*," Chrissie replied, already walking

away from them. She lifted her arm and waved without turning her head.

"Where are we going to meet?" Mark called.

"At the end of your block," Chrissie called back. "Nine o'clock. Don't be late."

And then, before either of them could say anything else, Chrissie had darted across the road through the traffic.

Mark had been looking forward to seeing her since the moment he had gotten up — and now she was gone. He felt strangely deflated.

"Some of the guys said they were going to be playing Frisbee down on the beach," Calvin suggested. "Want to go look for them?"

Mark nodded.

They might as well.

A haze of cloud hid the stars as the three of them made their way up out of the town that evening. Chrissie was carrying a black leather shoulder bag.

Mark's mother had been fine with him spending the night at Calvin's place. She trusted him so much that she didn't even think of phoning Calvin's parents to check out the story. Mark felt bad about lying to her; there was something particularly mean about deceiving someone who had complete faith in you.

Calvin hadn't had any problems, either. The two buddies often slept over at each other's houses. It was no big deal. And once the game was over, they would be able to creep in through the back door of Mark's house and slip up to his room undetected.

They left the last of the houses behind and walked down the narrow lane that ran along the crest of the hill. It was hemmed in by tall hedges — leaving only a dark slot of starless sky above their heads.

Mark was pretty certain that Chrissie had a snake hidden away in her shoulder bag. It was zipped up tight, and she was carrying it carefully. But he preferred not to ask her about it. His date with the snake would come soon enough. Better not to think about it for now.

But Calvin had other ideas.

"What's in the bag?" he asked as they filed along the lane.

"Mark's *destiny*," Chrissie said with a laugh.

"You've got a snake?" Calvin said. "Really? Where did you get it?"

"I imagine she borrowed it from that neighbor she told us about," Mark said, glad that he didn't sound as apprehensive as he felt. "The weirdo who keeps reptiles in the basement of the house she's staying in."

"Absolutely correct," Chrissie said.

"That's so cool," Calvin said. "What kind of snake is it?"

"A green one," Chrissie replied. "The weirdo named it Vampira."

"Is it poisonous?" Calvin asked.

Chrissie turned and looked at Mark with shining eyes. "Let's hope not, eh?" she said with a smile that almost made the upcoming ordeal seem worthwhile. "You are going to feel so great when you confront your fear of snakes. You'll be a total hero!"

A pent-up silence came down over them.

"This is it," Mark said a couple of minutes later. "The woods." The tall hedges were broken by a dilapidated wooden gate, held closed by a rusty chain.

Beyond the gate, there was a stretch of wild grassland before the densely packed trees.

"OK," Chrissie said. "Let's get this show on the road." She climbed the gate and jumped down on the other side.

Mark gave Calvin a quick look. He was staring at the trees with narrowed eyes.

"A bunch of trees are nowhere near as scary as a snake," Mark said under his breath. He grinned. "Maybe we can swap phobias."

Calvin gave a nervous laugh. "I don't think Chrissie would agree to that," he said.

They climbed the gate. The top bar was rotten, with mean-looking splinters and nails sticking out. Chrissie was already wading through the tall grass toward the edge of the woods. Heavy shadows lurked under the trees. There was no wind. The hilltop was almost silent. The only sound was the swish of their legs as they scythed through the grass.

Chrissie halted under the nearest tree. She carefully laid her bag on the ground, unzipped a small front pocket, and pulled out a length of twine and a strip of black cloth.

"OK," she said. "Who's first?"

Calvin stepped forward. Mark could see that he was

avoiding looking into the darkness under the trees. As much as Calvin had tried to convince them that his dislike of the woods was just based on a bad childhood incident, Mark could tell that he was finding this difficult. He might not want to admit it in front of a girl, but Calvin definitely had a phobia about that forest.

"Well done, Calvin," Chrissie said. "And because you volunteered, Mark goes first." She stooped again and unzipped the bag, stared into it for a few moments, then reached in.

Mark's heart pounded. All the hairs on his body stood up.

Her hand came up, and she was holding a snake in her fist. Mark guessed that the snake was about the length of his arm and not much thicker than his thumb. It coiled lazily in her hand, moving almost in slow motion. The long, flat head roved back and forth on the supple neck. Mark took an involuntary step backward as Chrissie straightened up. She held the creature at arm's length, a half-smile on her face as she watched it writhe and coil in the air.

"Isn't Vampira pretty?" she said.

She walked toward Mark. He struggled to stand his

ground. Every instinct in him was telling him to turn and run. And there was a look in Chrissie's eyes that frightened him. Forget the game — just get out of there. Calvin could have his sneakers. This wasn't worth it. But he didn't move. The blood was throbbing in his head. His arms were stiff, his hands clenched into painfully tight fists.

Chrissie stood in front of him. The snake had looped twice around her wrist. The head was rising and falling. The tongue flickered. It had eyes like black beads. Its shining coils were green and murderous-looking.

"Don't worry," Chrissie said, her voice soft and strangely gentle. "It isn't really poisonous. It won't hurt you." She stepped forward and unwound the snake from her wrist. "Trust me," she whispered.

Mark stood terrified as Chrissie draped the snake over his shoulders.

"I know stuff about snakes, and as far as I can remember, this one won't do much," she said dismissively. "It's too cold, and they are cold-blooded. It'll probably just go to sleep." She brushed his cheek with her fingers. Mark couldn't tell whether it was an accident or not.

Then she stepped back. "OK," she said more loudly. "If you touch the snake or do anything to try and get rid of it before I say so, you forfeit the game." She turned toward Calvin. "And now it's your turn."

Mark stood there in a world of nightmares. He could see the head and the tail of the snake, feel it moving slowly at the back of his neck — cold and smooth and sleek. He dreaded the moment when that small, wedge-shaped head would turn toward him and the mouth would open to reveal the needle-sharp fangs. He was only half aware of Chrissie binding Calvin's hands behind his back with the twine and wrapping the strip of cloth around his eyes.

"I'm going to lead you right into the woods," she told him. "Then I'm going to leave you there. If you call out for help, I'll come and get you — but you lose the game. If you try to take off the blindfold, you lose the game. Mark is going to be wearing the snake for the same length of time as I'm going to leave you in the woods. If either of you gives up, the other one wins. If you both keep it up, then I'll declare it a draw."

"After how long?" Calvin asked, and Mark felt some relief to hear that his friend's voice was trembling.

"That's for me to know, and you to find out," Chrissie said with a dangerous glint in her eye. Mark could tell that she was enjoying herself. She had them both in her control and she was loving every minute of it.

And with that, she pushed Calvin ahead of her under the trees. Mark lost sight of them in a matter of seconds. For a little while longer, he could hear their footfalls, then everything became silent.

He could feel the snake moving, its scales rubbing against the bare skin at the back of his neck. Its head reached out, wavering to and fro, the tongue flickering. Mark stared at it, not daring to move a muscle in case it suddenly turned and lunged at his neck. He could almost feel those fangs sinking into his flesh, injecting a murderous venom.

Chrissie had said it wasn't a poisonous snake, but what if she was wrong?

A hollow, frightened voice was echoing in his head: *Get it off me! Get it off!*

The snake looped itself loosely around his neck. Mark lifted his hands, ready to tear it off if the coil began to tighten.

Chrissie came walking out of the darkness under the trees.

"No touching it!" she warned him as she approached. "That's cheating."

"I don't care," Mark said, his voice a dry croak. "I'm not letting it strangle me."

"It won't," she said. She lifted a hand and ran a finger along the snake's body. "You expect them to feel slimy, don't you?" she said. "But they aren't. They're really quite silky."

Mark swallowed hard.

"For how long are you going to make us do this?" he asked.

She frowned. "I'm not *making* you do anything," she said. "It's the game. You play or you don't play. It's up to you. If you can't stand it, just take off the snake. I won't stop you."

Mark winced; the snake was beginning to tighten itself around his neck. It wasn't a problem yet, but he really didn't like the sensation.

Chrissie watched for a few moments as the snake slid across Mark's bare skin, her eyes bright and fascinated. Mark could feel cold sweat running down his face. Another second and he'd break! He couldn't stand this anymore.

Then, without a word, Chrissie reached out and carefully unwound the snake from his neck. She slid it off his shoulders and left him standing there in relief and confusion as she went over to the bag and put away the snake.

She walked back to him.

"You did it," she said. She moved suddenly toward him and gave him a quick kiss on the cheek.

Mark gave a breathless laugh, his face growing hot. He suddenly felt foolish for ever having believed that Chrissie would have put a poisonous snake on him.

"Maybe snakes aren't *so* bad," he said, gazing into her wide silver eyes. "I still hate them, though."

She smiled, then looked over her shoulder into the woods. "Should I go and get Calvin now?" she asked, a sly, amused tone coming into her voice. "Or should we leave him out there for a while longer?" She turned and looked at him, her eyes huge and bright in the darkness. "What do you think?"

Mark didn't know what to think. What did she mean? Was she suggesting that they keep Calvin blindfolded out in the woods until he cracked? Did she want to be alone with him for a bit longer?

He looked into her face, trying to figure her out.

After a moment, Mark said, "We can't leave him there."

Chrissie pouted and gave a curious little shrug. "OK," she replied.

She walked in under the trees. "Hey! Calvin!" she called. "Game over! I'm coming to get you!"

There was silence for a few moments, then Mark heard a shouting from deep in the woods. It was Calvin — and he sounded terrified.

Mark ran toward the woods. Calvin's yells filled the night. Chrissie was standing there, looking into the forest, but doing nothing.

Mark ran in under the trees, trying to pinpoint the direction from which the cries were coming.

"Calvin!"

A distant voice called back. "Mark!"

"I'm coming," Mark called, jogging toward the voice. "Keep shouting!"

He plunged into the darkness under the trees, pushing branches and undergrowth aside with his arms, listening for the sound of his friend's voice.

"Calvin?"

"Over here!" The voice still sounded panicky, but at least the terrified edge had gone.

Mark saw a dark shape in the gloom — stretched out on the ground. A pale face was turned toward him, the eyes covered with the black cloth. He kneeled down. There was some blood on Calvin's forehead, and his face was covered with dirt. He pulled off the blindfold. Calvin's eyes were wide with alarm.

"Get my hands free!" Calvin gasped. Mark quickly undid the knotted twine that bound his friend's wrists. Calvin sat up, panting and with his clothes covered in litter from the forest floor. He stared around with wide, frightened eyes. He was breathing hard, his eyes showing a blind panic.

Mark had never seen his friend like this before.

"What happened?" Mark asked as he helped Calvin to his feet.

"There's something in the woods," Calvin said. "I heard it coming toward me. Let's get out of here!"

"How did you cut yourself?" Mark asked.

"I think I ran into a low branch or something," Calvin said. "Is it bad?"

Mark looked at the cut. It was bloody, but not deep. "I think you'll live," he said. But something else was worrying him now. He had run into the woods without thinking — and now he wasn't certain of the way out. The darkness was confusing.

He took a huge breath. "Chrissie!" he called.

The deep dark silence of the forest surrounded them as they stood listening for a response.

"Chrissie!" he called again, even louder this time.

Nothing.

Mark frowned. Surely she must have heard him — so why didn't she answer?

He looked at Calvin. His friend had his back pressed up against a tree trunk. He was glancing all around, as if he sensed something coming for them.

"Are you OK?" Mark asked.

Calvin nodded. "I feel a little dizzy, that's all."

"I think I can figure out the way back."

They set off in what Mark hoped was the right direction. Although being in the woods didn't scare him, Calvin's panic was beginning to make him jumpy.

"I definitely heard something," Calvin said. Mark stared at him. This was beginning to freak him out — he had never seen Calvin so scared before.

"It was probably an animal of some kind," Mark replied. "Maybe a fox."

"I don't think so. It sounded too big."

Mark looked at Calvin. "You mean like a stray dog, or a . . . killer rabbit?" Mark asked with mock horror.

Calvin let out a splutter of laughter.

Mark grinned.

It was only a minute or so before they came out into the open. Mark was more than a little relieved. They were about twenty yards away from the gate where they had entered the woods.

"I think maybe you're right, and the thing in there was a dog or something," Calvin said with an embarrassed grin. "How was the snake?"

Mark shivered. "As creepy as the woods."

Calvin frowned. "Where's Chrissie?" he asked.

There was no sign of her. They walked along the

edge of the forest until they came to the spot where she had put down the black bag. It was no longer there.

Mark cupped his hands around his mouth and called into the trees. "Chrissie!"

Silence.

Had she followed him in there? Would he have to go and search for her?

"Hey — look," Calvin said.

Mark turned and stared in the direction in which his friend was pointing. "What?"

"The top of the gate is broken off."

Mark frowned. "She must have climbed back over," he said. That was the only answer. That bar had been fairly loose, but it would never have fallen away by itself; it would take the pressure of someone climbing over it to break it off.

Calvin stared at him. "She just left?" he said in disbelief. He looked at Mark. "What happened? Did she say anything?"

Mark shook his head. "She took off the snake," he said. "Then she called you. When I heard you shouting, I went to look for you. She was just standing there."

"Didn't she say anything?"

For some reason, he decided not to tell Calvin about the kiss — or that she had suggested they might leave him stranded in the woods. "I don't know what she's up to," Mark said bitterly. "She can just get lost for all I care. I've had it with her!"

They went back to Mark's place for the night. It wasn't as late as they had expected, and Mark's parents were still up. He told them that they had changed their minds about sleeping at Calvin's because his PlayStation wasn't working properly.

The cut on Calvin's forehead turned out to be a small scratch. It didn't even need a bandage. Calvin went straight to the bathroom and washed his face without Mark's mom and dad even noticing it.

Though they played a few games, neither of them was really in the mood, and it wasn't long before they gave up and went to bed. They didn't talk about Chrissie.

But Mark lay awake for quite a long time. He remembered what his mother had said: *Girls can be dangerous.*

He was beginning to believe her.

—

It was mid-morning before they finally got up and wandered down to the kitchen.

They had the house to themselves. Mark's parents were at work.

Mark put some bread in the toaster and poured two glasses of orange juice while Calvin set up the PlayStation in the living room. There was a big, wide-screen TV in there — much better than the small portable one Mark had in his room. And they could spread the cushions from the couch over the floor and make themselves really comfortable while they played.

Neither of them mentioned Chrissie, although Mark's head was still full of her. Calvin was strangely quiet, and Mark got the feeling that he was also think-ing about her — but he didn't say anything, so Mark didn't ask.

It was while they were digging into a large bag of Doritos and swigging orange juice from the carton that Calvin finally spoke.

"There's something I have to tell you," he said. "I wasn't going to — but . . ." His voice trailed off.

Mark knew instinctively that this was going to be about Chrissie.

"Go on," Mark said.

"Last night . . . when Chrissie took me into the woods," Calvin began, his voice hesitant and his eyes turned away. "She kissed me."

Mark felt a cold fist clench in his stomach.

"Only on the cheek," Calvin added quickly. "But then she said that if I wanted, she'd let me take off the blindfold. She said she'd make you keep the snake around your neck until you totally freaked out." He frowned. "It was like she wanted you to lose." Finally, he looked at Mark. "I told her it wasn't fair," he said. "So she just left me there with the blindfold still on."

There was a long silence. Mark couldn't believe it. Chrissie had made fools of them both.

"She did the same with me," Mark said at last. "She took the snake off me — and then she kissed me on the cheek and said we could leave you in the woods for a while, if I wanted to." He looked at Calvin. "I said no."

A look of bewildered anger came over Calvin's face. "What is it with that girl?"

"She likes to play games," Mark said angrily. "She was trying to turn us against each other."

"She's been messing with our heads right from the start," Calvin said. "Next time I see her, I'm going to tell her exactly what I think of her."

"I'm kind of hoping I don't see her again at all," Mark said.

There was another long pause in the conversation as both boys lapsed into their own silent thoughts.

"I liked her," Calvin said at last, his voice very quiet. "I sort of wish she wasn't like that."

"Me, too," Mark said, thinking of how amazingly cool she was.

And then the doorbell rang.

Mark got up and headed out into the hall and opened the door.

It was Chrissie.

Her T-shirt read:

You all laugh at me because I'm different.
I laugh at you because you're all the same.

"What do you want?" Mark asked, his voice harsh and bitter.

Chrissie seemed taken aback. "I thought you'd come down to the beach," she said. "I waited for you all morning." Her voice rose in a puzzling way. "What's wrong?"

Mark glared at her. "You don't know?"

She shook her head. "No, I really don't. What did I do?"

Calvin appeared behind him in the hallway. "We've had enough of you and your stupid games," he said. "Why don't you get lost?"

Chrissie gazed at him with her mouth fallen open. "Are you both crazy?" she said. She swallowed hard, her face crumpling with distress. "I thought we were going to be friends," she said in a choking voice. "I guess I was wrong." She turned and walked down the path.

"Wait!" Mark called. She stopped, half turning to look back at him. "Why did you disappear like that last night?" he asked angrily.

She looked surprised. "What?" She turned, frowning. "The game was over. You'd both beaten it. There was no reason to stay there. I was tired, so I went home. Why? Did you think I'd hang around there all night with you?"

"Calvin was hurt. You must have heard him shouting," Mark said.

She walked slowly back up the path, looking at Calvin. "Hurt how?"

"He fell — he cut his head."

"Show me."

"It's nothing," Calvin said. "It's just a small cut on my forehead." He glared at her. "What was all that last night — kissing us and trying to get us to cheat against each other? Don't deny it!"

"I wasn't going to deny it," Chrissie said. "That was part of the test — to see whether you'd sell each other out to win." She smiled. "Neither of you did. That was great. I was really impressed."

Mark stared at her, wishing he could see into her head and really get to know what was going on in there. Was she lying? It was really difficult to be sure of anything with her.

There was a heavy silence.

"Can I come in?" Chrissie asked. "Or do you both

hate my guts now?" Then she smiled and Mark smiled back, and suddenly everything seemed OK again.

He stepped aside to let her through.

She looked at Calvin. "Am I forgiven?" she asked.

"I suppose so," he said, and his face cleared. He shook his head. "Do you know you're a complete nut job?"

She laughed. "You have *no* idea," she said.

"We're playing a game called ZOMBEEZ," Calvin said. "Mark thinks you might be able to figure out why we keep getting killed. But I told him there's no way."

"Wanna bet?" Chrissie asked confidently. "Show me."

Calvin led Chrissie through into the living room. Mark closed the front door and followed them in. It seemed as though things were going to be just fine between them after all.

Chrissie sat cross-legged on a pile of cushions in the middle of the floor. She was leaning forward, staring at the TV screen as she manipulated the controller. Calvin sat to one side, rereading the ZOMBEEZ instruction book. Mark sat watching Chrissie, mesmerized by the intense concentration in her silver eyes.

The phone rang and Mark went to answer it.

It was Stuart — a classmate who was as into video-games as Calvin and Mark.

"Have you found the secret level on ZOMBEEZ yet?" Stuart asked.

"What secret level?" Mark said. "How do you find the code?"

A minute later, he was back in the living room with Calvin and Chrissie, breathlessly relaying the information while Chrissie manipulated the objects on the screen.

It didn't take Chrissie long to crack it. Within minutes, all three of them were gathered around the monitor as they took it in turns to play the elite level of the game. Chrissie took the controls and managed to beat them at the very last moment. The ZOMBEEZ were defeated, the solar system was safe again, and the game was over.

Mark had had an amazing afternoon. Things seemed to be working out with Chrissie the way he had hoped they would.

"That wasn't bad for a computer game," Chrissie said, leaning back on her pile of cushions and stretching. Mark and Calvin were on either side of her. "It doesn't compare with Who Dares Wins, of course," she added with a smile.

"Not that again," Calvin said, laughing. "Don't you ever give up with that game?"

"Listen," Chrissie said, looking from one to the other. "Didn't both of you like winning? So why don't we play one last round of the game?" She smiled. "Don't you want to know which one of you is the bravest?"

Mark looked suspiciously at her. He knew how tricky she could be when she was trying to get them to do what she wanted, but she did have a point. He and Calvin had gone along with her so far with that game. They had played two rounds and they had come out even. It would be good to find out if he could actually beat Calvin.

He looked at his friend. "I'm up for it if you are," he said.

Calvin was thoughtfully silent for a moment. Then he grinned. "If I win, do I still get your sneakers?" he asked.

"So long as I get your jersey," Mark agreed.

Chrissie clapped her hands, grinning from ear to

ear. "Great!" she said. "I've already worked out dares for both of you — and I know exactly where we should do it." She jumped up. "OK — I want you to meet me at the west end of Lincoln Avenue at half past four tomorrow morning."

Calvin stared at her. "That's the middle of the night!" he said.

Chrissie nodded. "It has to be that early, or it won't work." She smiled at them. "This is going to be so great!" she said. "I can't wait!" She headed for the door.

"Where are you going?" Mark said, not quite believing that she was rushing off again.

She looked at him. "I've got things to get ready," she said. "Remember — half past four tomorrow morning. Don't be late!" She slipped out of the room, and a few seconds later they heard the front door close.

"I've said it before," Calvin intoned, "and I'll say it again: That girl is nuts!"

Mark shook his head and grinned. "But like she said, at least we'll know which of us is the bravest," he said. "Uh — and that would be *me*, of course."

"In your dreams!" laughed Calvin. "I don't care what she comes up with — you're going to be *toast!*"

"Yeah, right! I really believe that!" Mark said. He looked at Calvin. "This place is nearer to Lincoln Avenue than your house," he said. "I guess you'll be sleeping over again."

Calvin laughed. "I suppose I will," he said. "I hope you've got a good alarm clock."

It was in the gray darkness before dawn that Calvin and Mark met up with Chrissie at the end of Lincoln Avenue. The occasional car swept by and the odd house light glowed, but it was eerily quiet in the town. It seemed to Mark that they were the only people out walking the streets.

Chrissie was sitting on a wall, wrapped in a black leather jacket several sizes too big for her, propped on her arms, swinging her legs, exactly like when they had first seen her down by the beach. As they approached, she jumped down. Mark saw that her black T-shirt had another slogan on it, spelled out in large white letters.

Stick around —
It gets worse.

"OK," she said. "As this is the final round of the game, the winner gets a special prize."

"What kind of prize?" Calvin asked.

Chrissie took two white envelopes from the inside pocket of the leather jacket. She handed one to each of them. Mark turned his over. It was sealed. Calvin's looked the same.

"You can't open them until I say so," Chrissie told them. "It's part of the game."

"Fair enough," Mark said. He folded the envelope in half and pushed it into his jeans pocket. "But you still haven't told us our dares."

"You'll find out," Chrissie said with a smile. "Come with me."

They followed her along the silent street. At the far end, Mark could see the tall yellow wooden panels that formed a high barrier around the building site where she had told them her father worked. Mark guessed that whatever she had planned for them, it would have something to do with that place.

Chrissie led them toward a pair of large plywood gates, held together by a chain and a padlock. Here, a panel had been cut to avoid a chunk of masonry that jutted out into the pavement. Whoever had cut the plywood had left a small gap.

Chrissie ducked down and wriggled through.

Calvin hesitated, staring down at the narrow slot.

"What?" Mark asked.

"Ever heard of trespassing?" Calvin said.

Chrissie's head appeared through the gap. "What's keeping you?" she asked.

"These places have surveillance cameras every-where," Calvin said. "We'll be seen."

"I don't think so," Chrissie said. "Trust me." She looked at Mark. "Trust me?" she said again.

Mark looked at her. Could they *really* trust her? If they wanted to play the game, they didn't really have much choice.

He crouched by the gap. Chrissie's head withdrew and he squeezed through. He stood up and looked around. There were overflowing Dumpsters nearby. Heaps of piping like ripped-out intestines. Raw steel girders. Enormous sacks of sand. Stack after stack of bricks. Cement mixers with hollow, gaping mouths.

Heavy machinery with crooked, jutting arms and jagged-toothed jaws that loomed against the sky like sleeping dinosaurs.

The main construction area was a little way off over a moonscape of rutted earth and crushed rubble. A basic framework of girders formed a web of steel against the sky — towering up to about ten yards, straddling a deep, dark pit with corrugated iron sides.

Mark shivered. Something about the place gave him the creeps. He felt a warm touch on his hand. He looked around. Chrissie was at his side, smiling at him, putting his hand in hers.

"It'll be fine," she said in a soft voice. "You'll see."

Her hand fell away from his as Calvin came crawling in through the gap.

"My dad tells me there are only four surveillance cameras for the whole site," Chrissie said, pointing. "I don't think they're going to be seeing much right now."

The nearest camera was fixed to a wooden post on the outer wall. It had a black plastic bag tied over it.

"They don't check the monitors till about half past seven," Chrissie explained. "By the time they realize someone's covered the cameras, we'll be done."

She picked her way across the site. Mark and Calvin followed her.

Chrissie stood at the brink of the dark pit. Calvin held back, but Mark stepped up next to her. It was difficult to be absolutely sure in the predawn gloom, but he guessed that the pit was probably about forty yards square and fifteen feet deep.

"My dad told me that they're going to pour the foundations soon," Chrissie said. "That's why we needed to do this right now — otherwise it'll be too late."

"What exactly are we supposed to do?" Calvin asked.

Chrissie smiled at him. "*You're* going to confront your fear of heights," she said. "And Mark is going to come face to face with his fear of confined spaces."

Calvin gave a snort of laughter. "If you think I'm going to go climbing around on those girders, you can think again," he said. "If I fall, I'll die. No way."

"You won't die," Chrissie said with a reassuring smile. "It's not that far down. And besides, you'll have a safety rope." She gestured with her hand, pointing to where four girders met out over the middle of the pit. "That's where you have to stand," she said.

Mark watched her. She was almost glowing with

excitement now, caught up completely in the rush of the game. There was something so cool about her when she was like this. It made him glad they had agreed to play this last round.

Calvin stared at the place where the girders intersected for a few long moments. "And what does Mark have to do?" he asked.

Chrissie turned and pointed to a large, battered old metal chest. "He has to go in there," she said. She walked over to the chest and crouched. There was a hasp on the front of the hinged lid, held closed by a large, rusty nail. She worked the nail loose and threw open the lid. The chest was half full of hard hats and fluorescent jackets and a few hand tools. She began to toss them out.

"But I won't be able to breathe," Mark said, a cold ripple of fear surging through his stomach.

"I'll fix that," Chrissie said. "Help me, will you?"

Between the three of them, they soon emptied the chest. Chrissie slammed the lid down. She picked up a heavy chisel and a club hammer. They watched as she hammered a series of ragged holes into the lid.

She stood up, panting from the effort. "There you

go," she said. "Airholes." She grinned. "You see? I thought of everything." She looked at them. "So? Are you up for this?"

Mark looked at Calvin. "I am if you are," he said to him.

"Who Dares Wins," Calvin said, looking challengingly into Mark's eyes. "Meaning me."

"I don't think so," Mark said. He looked at Chrissie. "We're ready," he said.

"One last thing," Chrissie told them. "It's important that you can see each other — so you know there's no cheating going on. The chest needs to be down in the pit." She looked at Mark. "So that you can see Calvin and he can see you. OK?"

"That sounds like a good idea," Mark said. Not that he believed that Calvin would cheat. But if he could actually see his friend suffering up there on the girder, it might make his own ordeal easier to cope with.

Chrissie smiled. "Off you go now — drag it over there and throw it down."

Mark grabbed one of the rusty handles on the side of the chest. Calvin took hold of the other. The chest was heavy but manageable. They got it to the edge of the pit and then heaved it over. It crashed down, landing the right way up but at an angle where its sharp edges had dug into the soft earth.

A metal ladder led down into the pit, roped at the top so it couldn't slip. Chrissie led the way down. She got Calvin and Mark to heave the chest into the middle of the pit. Mark looked around. There were walls of corrugated iron sheets that resembled some sort of futuristic slave pit in one of his videogames.

Chrissie pulled her leather jacket around herself as if feeling a sudden chill.

"OK," she began. "The rules are really simple. It's an endurance test. If either of you calls out that you've had enough, that's the end of the game. If *neither* of you calls out, I'll end the game after fifteen minutes and the whole thing will be a draw."

"And what happens if it's a draw?" Calvin asked.

"Then there'll be a tiebreaker," Chrissie said. "You'll find out what that is if it happens." She stooped and lifted the lid of the chest. She looked at Mark. "In you go," she said.

He climbed into the chest. It would be a tight fit — but not an impossible one. He lay down on his side, curling his legs up, propping himself on one elbow.

Chrissie looked down at him. "Just yell when you've had enough," she said. She leaned over him for a second and spoke in a private whisper. "I bet you win."

Mark looked up into her eyes, suddenly convinced that he really could do this.

She straightened up again. "'Bye for now!" she said aloud.

There was a final glimpse of her smiling face, and then the heavy metal lid came down with a piercing clang and everything went utterly dark. Mark heard scraping sounds as Chrissie forced the long nail in through the hasp, securing the lid in place.

Mark felt fear crawling through him as the reality of what he had agreed to do hit him for the first time. He was locked helplessly in the chest. In those first few moments, it felt as if the sides of the chest were closing in around him like a deadly, squeezing fist. But as he lay there on the cold metal, his eyes began to adjust to the darkness. He could see points of gray light above him — the jagged holes that Chrissie had cut in the lid.

He drew himself up as high as he could and peered

through one of the larger holes. He could see the network of girders above him: narrow black lines against a sky that was just beginning to brighten with a cold, steely dawn light.

"Hello?" he called. "Anyone there?"

But there was no reply. He shivered, suddenly very alarmed. What if they just abandoned him there?

Calm down! They aren't going to do that!

He squirmed around in the confines of the chest, trying to get a better view of the outside world. He found a hole that let him see the side of the pit with the long ladder. He saw that Chrissie and Calvin were already up at ground level. Chrissie was tying a length of rope around Calvin's waist. It was too far for Mark to see his friend's expression, but he guessed that Calvin must be getting really panicked by now.

Mark had flashbacks of when they were younger. Calvin bug-eyed and gray-faced with fear at the top of a Ferris wheel. Or of him freaking out when they leaned from a top-floor window in an office building during a school trip. The pit wasn't actually that deep, but Mark knew that Calvin would feel as though the ground was miles away.

Oddly, Mark felt quite calm. So far. The airholes allowed him to concentrate on things outside the chest — they helped take his mind off the fact that he was locked in there. But the metal was very cold. The chill ate right through his clothes.

He watched as Chrissie walked out onto the girder, stretching her arms out to either side for balance and with the end of Calvin's safety rope in her hand. She had looped it around a pulley nearby and then tied it around Calvin's waist. She tip-toed to a place where four girders met. It was directly above Mark's head. He could hardly make her out now.

Mark could hear her voice. "OK," she called. "Walk toward me. Don't look down — feel ahead with your feet. Keep your eyes on me. I won't let you fall. Trust me."

Calvin climbed onto the girder and began walking slowly. Mark watched as his friend inched his way forward, clutching the rope.

"That's good," Chrissie called, looping the rope in her hands as he approached her. "You're doing fine."

"That's what you think." Mark could hear a tremble in his friend's voice.

Now Calvin had come to the intersection, and Mark could only see him as a strange, foreshortened black shape against the gray sky. Then he saw Chrissie step around him from girder to girder and walk slowly back the way they had come, feeding out the rope as she went.

She came to the edge of the pit. She sat down astride the girder, gathering up the slack in the rope.

She looked at her watch. "OK," she called. "Game on!"

Just fifteen minutes and it would be over. Mark's arms and legs were beginning to feel cramped and uncomfortable. He shifted around in the chest, trying to get into a position where he could see out without straining his neck or twisting his arms and legs into awkward, painful knots. The fear of being in the chest was still with him, but it was balanced against his determination to beat Calvin.

He wished he'd thought to bring a watch. It was difficult to guess at how the time was passing. He tried counting out the seconds, but he kept losing track — his mind was too distracted for that. The cold was beginning to bite into him, and as the time dragged by, he became more and more aware of how small and dark the chest really was. He couldn't stretch his legs out at all. He couldn't sit up; the lid pressed down too close. The only position that was even remotely comfortable was on his side, with his knees curled up to his stomach and his arms wrapped around himself. But in that position, the airholes were far away.

After only a short time, he began to feel breathless and dizzy. He lifted his face up to the lid again and put his mouth to one of the holes, sucking air into his lungs.

He heard Chrissie calling. "Hey, Mark? How are you doing?"

"Not too bad!" he called back, hoping he sounded more positive than he felt.

"That's great," Chrissie called. "Calvin? You OK?"

"Not really." Calvin sounded really scared up there.

"You'll be fine. Just don't look down," Chrissie said, her voice bright and encouraging. "You're both doing great."

Mark peered up through a hole. He could make out Calvin's jet-black shape up there where the four girders met. His arms were stretched out, thin black lines against a sky that was now silver-gray with the coming day.

Mark fell back, his shoulder and elbow aching from the effort of holding himself in that position. The feeling of airlessness came over him again. He began to pant, his heart hammering painfully in his chest. He could feel panic rising in him.

He strained up again, his eye to the hole. Surely he'd been in there for ten minutes by now. Or maybe it was only five minutes. He realized that he had no idea.

The sun was definitely up, but the pale white light was cold and cheerless.

He had to distract himself somehow. He reached around and pulled the folded envelope out of his back pocket. He held it close to a hole. What was inside? A prize for the winner — a forfeit for the loser. But what?

"Not long to go now, guys," Chrissie called. "Keep it up."

The sides of the chest seemed to be closing in on him — the lid was bearing down, squeezing all the air out, suffocating him. And suddenly, he didn't care about winning the game — suddenly, the only thing in the world that he wanted was to get out of there.

He was about to shout when he heard a call from Calvin.

"OK! I give up. Mark wins. I've had it!"

Mark strained up again, his eye against the hole. He could see that Calvin had come down on to his hands and knees on the girder — that he was clutching the edges with both hands.

Chrissie was leaning forward, looking at him.

"Are you sure?" she called.

"Yes! Get me off here!"

She got to her feet. Her voice was high and shrill as she shouted across to him. "Told you so!"

Mark was confused. Told them what?

What did she mean?

But then all other thoughts were beaten out of his mind as he saw Chrissie take the safety rope in both hands and give it a fierce tug.

Mark saw Calvin dragged forward. Chrissie gathered the rope in her hands and braced herself, grimacing with the effort, leaning backward till the rope was taut.

She pulled on it again, using all her weight this time. Calvin was slipping from the edge of the girder.

"Mark!" Calvin called in stark terror. "Please — help me!"

Mark twisted onto his back and tried to kick the lid open with his cramped legs. But it was hopeless. The lid didn't move. Mark forced his eye up to the hole again, desperate to help Calvin, kicking furiously but knowing there was absolutely nothing he could do. He watched in horror as his friend hung from his hands directly above him. Chrissie gave a final heave on the rope, and Calvin's hands came loose.

Calvin let out a scream. *"Ma-ark!"*

"No!" Mark shouted.

For a split second, he watched as his friend plummeted down toward him. There was a deafening, sickening bang as Calvin hit the lid of the chest. Mark screamed in terror as the lid caved in on him. A blazing pain erupted in his head.

Then everything went black.

Gradually, Mark became aware of two things. There was a terrible, throbbing pain in his head. And a voice was calling to him. He tried to move, but his feet hit the end of the chest. Then he remembered where he was. And he remembered what had happened to Calvin. It had been a long fall. Was Calvin badly hurt?

Chrissie's cheery voice came from nearby. "Hey, Mark — are you awake in there?"

The lid of the chest was deeply buckled in, and a long jagged split had opened across it. The light was shifting above him. He struggled to focus. He saw a wide slice of Chrissie's face as she stared down at him through the slit.

"Are you OK?" she asked, sounding concerned. "Boy — for a minute there, I thought he'd flattened you like a bug. Mark? Are you all right?"

"What happened to Calvin?" he coughed, too dazed at that moment to feel anger or fear — although deep in his mind both emotions were beginning to grow.

"He's right here," Chrissie said. "Did you see the way he came down? Wham! It was awesome!"

Mark's voice was dull — bewildered. "What did you do?" As he said the words, he heard a scuffling as his friend's body rolled off the top of the chest, and then a low, pained moan. A flood of relief washed over him. Calvin was alive. From the sound of it, he was hurt, and in a good deal of pain — but at least he was alive.

Mark suddenly realized how terrified he had been for a moment, imagining what could have happened to his best friend. And it was all Chrissie's fault. He slammed his fists against the lid of the chest. "How could you do that?" he shouted. "You could have *killed* him!"

Chrissie's face came closer to the slit, so that he could see her eyes staring down at him. "Don't be like that, Mark — it was just the game." She smiled. "You can open the envelope now. The game's over."

Mark beat the lid with his fist. "Let me out!" he shouted.

Chrissie's face moved away as she stood up. "No can do," she said.

Mark smashed his fists against the lid of the chest. It shuddered but held solid. He kicked at the end, his ears ringing with the dull metallic clangs of his shoes. But the sides didn't give so much as an inch.

"Open the lid, Chrissie!" Mark called.

"Not gonna happen!" came her happy voice.

Mark slammed his hands against the lid, wasting his

energy in a futile attempt to force it open. He slid his fingers through the slit, trying to make it wider — but the pain of pressing against the raw edges of metal was too much and when he pulled back, there was blood from deep cuts on his fingers.

He realized that Chrissie hadn't said anything in several minutes, and a stab of terror shot through him. What if she had left?

"Chrissie?" he called.

After a moment, she appeared, looming over the chest. She was smiling to herself, as though enjoying a private joke. Mark felt a cold dread come over him as he looked at her.

"Have you opened the envelope yet?" she called back.

"No." Mark had to fight to keep the hysteria out of his voice. "No, not yet. Chrissie? Will you let me out, please?"

"You should open the envelope," she said. "It explains everything."

"Please, Chrissie. Let me out."

She ignored him, humming a cheerful little song to herself.

He lay back, trying to think.

Chrissie was insane. Waves of ice-cold terror shot through his body. He felt as if he was living a nightmare. She was insane and she had almost killed his best friend.

He had to try to find a way of persuading her to let him out of the chest.

"Chrissie?" he called, his voice shaking. "OK — I'll open the envelope."

Maybe if he did that, she'd release him.

He felt for the envelope. His groping fingers found it under his leg.

Hideously uncomfortable, he managed to squirm into a position where he could hold the envelope up near to the light. He tore it open with shaking hands. Inside was a single piece of paper.

"Good," she said. "I have to go now."

"Chrissie? Don't go."

"I've got to," she said. "Don't worry, the construction workers will find you soon enough." She started to giggle. "Oh, it's Saturday, isn't it? Silly me!" Her voice already sounded distant. "Hope you don't have any plans till Monday."

"Please, Chrissie!" Mark shouted at the top of his voice. "*Chrissie!*"

He saw Chrissie climbing the ladder out of the pit. At the top, she turned and waved. She was smiling. Then she walked away and disappeared.

Mark let out a groan. She was right — someone would find them. Eventually. But who knew how long it would be? What if they were stuck down here for days? Maybe Calvin would go find help — if he was in any condition to do anything at all.

Mark was trapped. He could shout and shout until his voice gave out, but no one would hear him. The darkness grew heavier, closing in on him, and he bit his lips to stifle a scream. *I can't*, Mark thought in terror. *I can't stay here, not for another day, not for another hour. I'll go insane.*

Maybe Chrissie will come back, he told himself. *Maybe it was all just a joke that went horribly wrong.*

He realized he was still holding her letter — would it help him figure out what had happened? Would it give him some clue that would help him escape?

With trembling fingers, he unfolded the piece of paper, holding it to the small beams of light.

On it were written eight words in big capital letters. Eight words that almost stopped Mark's heart:

BELIEVE ME NOW?
GIRLS ALWAYS WIN.
<u>YOU</u> LOSE.

DON'T WAKE
THE BABY

"Alice! Phone!"

Alice Buchanan's fingers paused on the keyboard. It was seven thirty at night, and she was hurrying to finish her creative writing assignment so that she could go down to the living room and watch her favorite TV show.

"Who is it?" she shouted.

"Mrs. Wilkins," her mother called up the stairs.

"Coming!" Alice quickly saved the document and ran to her bedroom door. Mrs. Wilkins had put an advertisement in the local newspaper two weeks ago — "Reliable Babysitter Wanted."

Alice raced down the stairs and picked up the receiver. "Hello?" she panted. "This is Alice."

"Hello, Alice," came Mrs. Wilkins's brisk, teacherly voice. "Are you still interested in the babysitting job?"

"Yes — when would you like me to start?" Alice asked eagerly.

"Mr. Wilkins and I were hoping to go out on Friday night. We'd only be gone for three or four hours at most. Would you be able to manage that?"

"No problem," Alice replied.

"Could you be here by seven thirty?" Mrs. Wilkins asked.

"On the dot!" Alice said, looking for a pen and piece of paper to take down the Wilkinses' address. "Got it," she said.

"See you then," Mrs. Wilkins said. "Good-bye, Alice."

"Bye." Alice grinned as she put the phone down. She was excited about having her first babysitting job — *finally* she'd have the money to buy those jeans she wanted.

———

The car drew up in front of the Wilkinses' house.

"What time did they say they'd be back?" Alice's mother asked.

"Half past eleven — at the latest," Alice said, peering into the mirror on the sun visor. She wanted to make a good impression on the Wilkinses. She pushed her fingers through her long black hair, carefully rearranging the bangs that came down to her eyebrows.

"And you're sure they'll drive you home?" Alice's mom asked sternly.

"Yes, Mom," Alice said, exasperated. "I'll be fine." She winked at her mom and smiled. "And tomorrow morning, you can take me shopping!"

Alice got out of the car and watched her mother drive away. The thought of the coming evening was exciting, but also a little unnerving. She hoped that Mr. and Mrs. Wilkins would like her. After all, they had never actually met. Alice's only contact with them had been speaking with Mrs. Wilkins on the phone. She hoped she'd be able to cope with the baby. Taking a deep breath, Alice pushed her nerves to the back of her mind and focused on coming across as grown-up and competent.

The Wilkinses' home was one of a row of similar houses set on a hill behind broad, sloping front yards. The wooden gate creaked on its hinges as Alice pushed through, and the path to the house was cracked and uneven. She noticed that the plants in the front garden were a bit scraggly, and that the grass patches were overgrown with weeds.

The house itself was two stories high, with small windows that looked as though the frames could do with a fresh coat of paint. An uninviting, yellowish light shone from one upstairs window and through the downstairs bay. The front porch was unlit. At first glance, it seemed a sad, neglected kind of a place.

Alice climbed the steps to the front door and rang the bell. It made a harsh, electronic noise. After a moment, the door swung open. A tall, thin man with thick, horn-rimmed glasses stood there — Alice assumed it was Mr. Wilkins. His hair was short, pulled back off his forehead, and slicked down with some kind of gel. He had a long face and rather narrow, hunched shoulders. She guessed he must be in his mid-thirties. There was a splotchy brown birthmark on his right cheek, about the size of a penny. Alice tried hard not to stare at it.

"Right on time!" he said, smiling. "Please come in." He lowered his voice as she stepped into the hall. "Mrs. Wilkins is just putting Ralphie to sleep," he said, pressing a finger to his lips. The door banged shut behind Alice, startling her a little. She hadn't even seen Mr. Wilkins touch it.

Then Alice noticed an odd, musty smell in the hallway, as if the house needed airing out. She tried not to wrinkle up her nose in disgust. The wallpaper was dark and old-fashioned, and the hall was lit by a feeble bulb hanging in a shade that needed the cobwebs dusted off it.

"Please, after you," Mr. Wilkins said, rubbing his hands together and nodding toward a door. Alice pushed it open and led the way into the living room. Mr. Wilkins glided quietly in behind her. Some kind of weird orchestral music was coming from an old-fashioned wooden radio on the sideboard.

Alice gazed around the room in surprise. It had been decorated in a retro style, with old furniture and intricate, floral wallpaper. Even the pictures on the walls and the ornaments on the mantelpiece fit the fashion perfectly. It looked to Alice exactly like pictures from the 1950s she had seen in her grandmother's old photo album.

"Mrs. Wilkins will be down in a moment," Mr. Wilkins said. "Ralphie is teething," he went on. "It can make him cranky and bad-tempered. We have an awfully hard time getting him to sleep some nights." He lifted a finger, his head tilted as though listening, his eyes raised toward the ceiling behind their thick lenses. "Listen."

Alice listened for a few seconds. "I can't hear anything," she said.

Mr. Wilkins nodded, smiling cheerfully and rubbing his hands again. "I think he's gone to sleep at last. Mrs. Wilkins will be down in a moment or two."

Mr. Wilkins moved over to the radio and bent forward as if to listen more closely. He hummed for a moment and made tick-tock movements with his fingers, as if conducting. He smiled. "Do you like music, Alice?"

She nodded, quickly deciding that it wouldn't be a

good idea to tell him what she thought about *that* kind of music.

"Everyone likes music, Edmund," said a voice that made Alice jump. Mrs. Wilkins had come into the room without a sound and was standing behind her.

She was almost as tall as her husband, and if anything, even thinner, with hollow-looking cheeks and piercing, deep-set eyes. She was wearing a floral print dress and a yellow cardigan, and her dark hair was stiff with hair spray.

"Alice, how nice to meet you," Mrs. Wilkins said. "I hope Mr. Wilkins has been making you feel at home. We love having company."

"Yes, thanks," Alice said, trying hard to settle her nerves after the shock of Mrs. Wilkins's sudden appearance. "This is an amazing room," she said, hoping she sounded calm and capable. "It must have taken you ages to find all this stuff."

"I'm sorry, Alice, what do you mean?" Mrs. Wilkins asked, frowning.

"The 1950s look," Alice said nervously. "It's really . . . unusual."

Mr. and Mrs. Wilkins stared at her blankly.

"I'm sorry, Alice — I don't know what you mean," Mr. Wilkins said.

"Oh. Sorry. It doesn't matter," Alice said. She felt a hot flush of embarrassment redden her cheeks. So the retro stuff wasn't a "look" — it was just the way they were.

That was when it dawned on Alice that Mr. and Mrs. Wilkins had gone all the way with the retro style. It wasn't just the furniture and the decor that was from another time — their clothes, their hair, everything about them dated from fifty years ago.

Great start, Alice, she thought. *Keep it up, and you'll get fired before they walk out the door.*

"Is the little one asleep?" Mr. Wilkins asked his wife.

She smiled. "Like a lamb."

"What should I do if he wakes up?" Alice asked. "Is there a bottle I can give him, or should I walk him around for a bit?"

"Oh, he won't wake up," Mrs. Wilkins replied. "You won't get a peep out of him now — just so long as you don't make too much noise." She frowned. "You won't be noisy, will you, Alice?"

"Not a peep," Alice said. "I'll just sit and watch TV with the volume down really low." She glanced around the room, looking for the TV.

"I'm afraid we don't have a television," Mr. Wilkins said. "We find the wireless gives us all the entertainment we need."

Alice stared at him. *The what?* He was looking over toward the big old radio set. "Oh," she said. "OK. No problem. I'll just listen to the . . . um . . . radio, then." The odd couple were beginning to register on Alice's weirdometer. *Wireless?* Who uses words like *wireless* to describe a radio?

Mrs. Wilkins moved over to the sideboard and pointed to a door. "There are games and puzzles and magazines in there, if you get bored," she said.

"I'll be fine," Alice said, forcing a smile and wishing she'd thought to bring her MP3 player or a book.

"Well, dear," Mr. Wilkins said to his wife, pushing back the sleeve of his jacket and looking at his watch. "We should get going."

"Going anywhere nice?" Alice asked.

"We'll be back by eleven thirty," Mrs. Wilkins said, seeming not to have heard her.

"OK," Alice said. "But I still don't know what to do if Ralphie wakes up." There was an unsettled feeling in the pit of her stomach.

"He shouldn't now," Mrs. Wilkins said. "Just so long as you stay nice and quiet down here." She looked sternly at Alice. "Now, this is very important. Under no circumstances are you to go upstairs. Ralphie is a light sleeper, and the slightest sound can wake him up."

"But . . . what if he wakes up on his own?" Alice persisted, worried by the warning. "What if he starts crying?"

"He shouldn't now," Mrs. Wilkins said again. She pointed to a large, clunky old baby monitor that was perched on the edge of the sideboard. "Let's listen."

Alice listened. She heard soft, contented snuffling sounds over the crackle and hum of the monitor.

"OK, then," she said, feeling defeated.

"We'll be back by eleven thirty," Mrs. Wilkins reiterated. "The kitchen is along the hall. Make yourself something to eat. There's bread and cheese if you get hungry."

"Great — thanks." *Bread and cheese!* she thought. *Big deal!*

"The number of the place we're going to is beside the telephone, should you need to reach us," Mr. Wilkins said. They filed out into the hallway and stood for a moment.

There was a coat rack on the wall, and Alice waited for the Wilkinses to put on their coats. But they didn't move. After what felt like ages, Mr. Wilkins spoke.

"Front door, Alice," he said, nodding toward it. "If you please."

She gave him a puzzled look. "Oh, right. Of course." She walked to the door and pulled it open. She guessed they must be the kind of people who think it's good manners for young people to open and close doors for them.

The Wilkinses walked past her, arm in arm, and headed down the path. At the gate, Mrs. Wilkins turned and waved. Alice waved, and then swung the door shut.

They were gone. Alice puffed out her cheeks and blew a relieved breath. *Talk about weird,* she thought.

She gazed around the dimly lit hallway. It didn't seem so cold in the house now that they'd gone.

Alice listened intently. There was no sound from upstairs. She climbed the first three or four steps and listened again, her hand on the banister.

The house was absolutely silent.

Alice retreated into the living room. She picked up her bag and dug out her cell phone. She had promised to call her best friend, Emily, to let her know how it was all going.

She had to tell Emily about this place — and those unbelievable people! Talk about living in a world of their own! Alice switched off the awful radio music, then hit the SPEED DIAL buttons on her phone, followed by the green DIAL key. She put the phone to her ear, but there was no sound. Frowning, she tried again, but the phone was dead.

"Oh, great," Alice said sighing, "I forgot to charge the battery. That's just *perfect*." She glanced over to the phone on the sideboard. *I'm sure they won't mind me making a quick call,* she said to herself. *I'll give Emily this number, and then she can call me back.*

She lifted the heavy receiver and put it to her ear.

There was a crackling, hissing noise instead of a dial tone. Alice twirled the heavy plastic disc of numbers on the receiver a couple of times. The crackling came and went — but there was still no tone.

She glanced at the small slip of paper that lay by the side of the phone. There was some faded writing on it and three letters, printed out in capitals — and then four numbers. And the scrap of paper was browned and curled-up. The paper looked really old, and the ink appeared to be faded.

Alice frowned. Mrs. Wilkins had said that they'd left a telephone number for her — but that couldn't be it, surely? Confused, she looked again at the telephone. Next to the finger holes were both numbers and letters. The 2 had ABC next to it, 3 had DEF . . . and so on all the way around the disc. The phone itself was heavy and pretty old-fashioned, but it seemed to fit perfectly with the rest of the house.

"Not that it makes much difference," she muttered under her breath. "Modern or retro, the stupid thing is broken, anyway!" And then she stopped. What if the Wilkinses thought that she had broken the phone? Maybe it was an antique!

Alice ran into the hall. She had to try to catch the Wilkinses before they disappeared — she had to tell them that the phone wasn't working.

Alice opened the front door and stepped out onto the porch. In the darkness of the evening, the street lamps allowed her to see all the way down the road. The Wilkinses were nowhere to be seen.

"Oh, fantastic!" Alice muttered. The wind had picked up, and it was getting chilly. Night was gathering under the tall trees and in darkened doorways.

She shivered, trying to think what to do.

Don't panic, Alice thought. *This isn't a catastrophe.* She turned and stepped back into the house, quietly closing the door behind her. Alice looked at her watch. Eight o'clock. As long as Ralphie stayed asleep for the next three and a half hours, there should be no problems. But there was a nagging doubt burning away in the back of her mind.

What if he didn't?

Surely there had to be a bottle or *something* in the kitchen — something she could give him in an emergency if he woke up and started howling.

She walked down the hallway, alongside the stairs.

"I don't believe this," Alice breathed as she came into the kitchen. If anything, it was more perfectly set in the past than the living room. There was a heavy, dark wood cabinet with shelves on which patterned plates sat, and an old-fashioned porcelain sink in the far corner under something that she recognized as an ancient copper-colored water heater. The fridge was a small, dumpy thing. She couldn't even see a dishwasher or a microwave. It was like being in some kind of bizarre museum.

The weirdness of the house began to gnaw at her.

They must feed something normal to the baby, she said to herself.

She found some things in a cabinet under the wooden counter. There was a box of crackers. Alice took it out. As she opened it, an unpleasant smell hit her. The crackers were green with mold.

Alice put the box in the old garbage can near the door and walked over to the fridge. She had to yank at the handle to get it open. What confronted her was a mold-infested jungle of ancient-looking food.

"That is *so* disgusting!" Alice said out loud, holding her nose as she looked through the ancient, congealed milk, the green cheese, and the papery-looking ham. The vegetables at the bottom of the fridge were barely recognizable. Shutting the fridge door, she looked in the wooden bread box, only to find an uncut loaf that was as solid as a brick.

Alice shuddered, deciding that she wouldn't be making herself any sandwiches. She had imagined herself being given the run of a well-stocked fridge for the evening. The lack of anything decent — or even anything that wasn't moldy and disgusting — to eat was unbelievable! What *was* it with these people?

"What do they feed Ralphie?" Alice wondered aloud. "He must eat *something*." She opened more cabinets, but there was no sign of any baby food. Alice felt unease creep up her spine. Maybe the Wilkinses kept Ralphie's stuff upstairs? Wondering, she went back to the living room. What she needed to do now was to find something to pass the time till eleven thirty, so that she stopped thinking about how weird this whole evening was.

She turned on the radio. A few seconds later, more hideous orchestral music sounded from the speaker.

"No thanks," Alice said. She twisted the dial. There was a scratchy noise, but she couldn't find any other stations. She tried to get back to the original station, but that seemed to have disappeared as well. She listened to the irritating electronic crackling for a few moments, then switched the thing off.

She walked over to the window and drew the corner of the curtain open. No TV, no computer, no real radio stations, no working phone, no stereo, no food — nothing. This house reminded Alice of a pretend home in a Hollywood studio — it didn't seem to have anything real or functional in it.

Alice walked over to a cabinet and opened the door. There were two shelves — the top one stuffed with papers and magazines and the bottom one stacked with games in ratty, faded boxes.

Alice took the games out and stared at them. Monopoly. Chess. Chutes and Ladders. Something called "Totopoly," which she'd never heard of, but seemed to involve horse racing. She also found a few jigsaw puzzles and a deck of cards. In the shadows at the back of the shelf, she noticed that there was a book among the other things. It was a hardcover, with a thick leather binding. The title swept across the front cover in gold letters: *Joyful Memories*.

It was a photo album. Intrigued, Alice opened it. The earliest photos looked like antiques; pictures that captured people in curious clothes, inhabiting a forgotten, monochrome world.

Alice turned the thick card pages carefully. She came to some pictures of a baby on a rug. On the next page were pictures of a toddler with a baby.

There was old-fashioned writing under one of the pictures: "Our Two Little Treasures — Edmund and Howard. May 1931." *Edmund?* Alice thought. *Mr. Wilkins must have an older relative with the same name.*

There were pictures of other people, and other places — of holidays, and special occasions. She came across some Christmas photos. One showed a decorated tree, and paper streamers and balloons — and two small children sitting in the middle of a lot of torn wrapping paper. One of them must have been about four, holding up a model train.

Alice turned the page. There was a picture of the same boy in a school uniform. He was about eleven years old, she guessed, and was now wearing weird old, steel-rimmed round glasses. And then Alice noticed something that made her skin crawl. At first, she thought that it was an ink spot on the old photo, but as she stared more closely, she realized that it wasn't. It was a birthmark that looked like a rusty stain.

Or an old penny.

It was the same mark that Mr. Wilkins had on his cheek! The boy *had* to be Mr. Wilkins. *But he couldn't be.* Alice flipped back through the pages, scrutinizing the pictures, and she realized that the boy had the birthmark in every picture — the images were so old and grainy that she hadn't noticed before. *But it can't be the same Edmund*, she thought. *These photos are ancient!*

She went back to that first page, where there was a picture of the toddler and the baby, and the writing, "Our Two Little Treasures — Edmund and Howard. May 1931." 1931? Either the date had been written down wrong, or Mr. Wilkins would have to be over seventy years old now, and he was definitely not *that* old! The feeling of unease she'd experienced in the kitchen was returning now.

Alice tried to rationalize what she had seen, but she couldn't help feeling more and more creeped out.

She scrambled up, the photo album slipping to the floor. She had to get to a phone and call home.

Running out into the hall, Alice heard the baby monitor crackle into life back in the living room.

She froze, listening in dismay to the hiccuping cries.

Ralphie was awake.

All Alice wanted to do was to get out as quickly as possible — but she couldn't abandon a crying baby. She *couldn't.*

"Go back to sleep!" she said breathlessly, staring up the stairs. "Don't do this to me! *Please*, Ralphie — just go back to sleep!"

But the crying didn't stop. It got louder — more insistent and continuous.

Alice ran and picked up the phone, praying that it would be working again. The same useless crackling sound came from the receiver.

Frantically, she checked her cell phone again. It was still dead.

A cold panic began to take hold of her. What should she do?

Ralphie's crying was so loud now that she could hardly think. The piercing screams seemed to be invading her head, confusing her thoughts. Alice made a decision. She would go up and fetch him — then she would get out of this house with the baby in her arms and go next door for help.

Taking a deep breath, Alice ran up the stairs into the darkness of the landing.

The crying was coming from a door at the far end of the hallway. Alice walked quickly along and, in the gloom, she could just make out the bathroom on her left. A damp, unpleasant smell was coming from it.

Alice reached the door where the noise was coming from. "It's OK, Ralphie — I'm coming," she called. Cold, stale air brushed her face as she opened the door to the darkened room. At that moment, her fear was over-taken by the shock of seeing the conditions that Ralphie was being kept in. *How could they let a baby sleep in an unheated room like this?* Alice felt for a switch, and the room was suddenly wrapped in a dull, yellowish light. It was bare — uncarpeted and empty — except for a large crib with high wooden sides that stood right in the middle of the floor, directly under the weak, naked lightbulb.

Alice stepped into the room. Ralphie was howling now, his cries making her wince as she walked toward the crib. The door swung closed behind her, the rusty hinges sounding like fingernails scraping down a blackboard.

"Don't cry, Ralphie!" Alice called out, her voice a little shaky. "Alice is here. Don't cry — that's a good boy."

Then she saw something protruding from the crib. It was a length of wire. Alice followed it with her eyes across the floor and up to a plug that was inserted into a wall socket.

What parent would put something electrical in with a baby? Alice thought. *What could it be for?*

She leaned over the crib. Ralphie was tucked in under the covers — all she could see was the thin brown hair on the top of his head. The crying didn't stop, and Alice began to feel really scared. Ralphie wasn't moving, and she was sure that something was seriously wrong.

She reached out a hand to stroke his head. But what she touched was soft and squishy under her fingers. Alice pulled her arm away in alarm, shocked by the inhuman feel of the baby's head.

Her hand trembling, she reached down into the crib and drew back the covers.

The head fell sideways and rolled off the pillow.

Alice's heart crashed against her ribs. She stood there, rooted to the spot, unable to move, hardly able to breathe. Sweat began to mat her hair to her temples.

Then in an instant, relief washed over her. She saw that it was an old plastic doll's head — not that of a baby.

She threw the covers all the way back and stared in disbelief.

The covers hid a machine of some kind. Alice looked closer, and she could see that it was an old-fashioned tape recorder. A reel of tape was slowly winding from one spool to another. The crying was coming from an old metal speaker on top of the machine.

There was no baby.

Stunned and bewildered, Alice reached into the crib and pressed the STOP lever.

The crying ended abruptly, but Alice found the ensuing silence more terrifying.

Where was Ralphie?

Was there a Ralphie?

She tried to come to terms with what she had discovered. The Wilkinses had hired her to look after a baby that didn't even *exist*. Suddenly, the odd couple weren't just weird and a little eccentric. Alice had a terrible feeling that it was much stranger than that. They had lured her to this house . . . but why?

A bitingly cold wind struck Alice from behind, making the skin crawl on the back of her neck and down her arms.

She spun around and saw Mrs. Wilkins come drifting in through the open door. Alice screamed. Mrs. Wilkins's feet were hovering just above the ground.

"Oh, Alice," Mrs. Wilkins said. "We told you not to come up here. We told you not to wake the baby. You young people never listen. We just want some company, some life in this old house, and Ralphie was all we had — until now."

Mrs. Wilkins lifted her arm, her hand reaching out like a claw toward Alice.

"Don't touch me!" Alice screamed, and she lunged sideways, avoiding Mrs. Wilkins's grasping hand by a fraction of an inch. Desperately, she raced along the hallway, her heart in her mouth, her brain spinning.

"Yes, we always did want a daughter," said Mr. Wilkins, standing at the head of the stairs, blocking her path. A smile stretched across his face as he beckoned to her with a long, slender finger.

Alice threw herself at a closed door along the landing.

Please let it be unlocked!

The door burst open with a creak of ancient hinges, and Alice raced through it, slamming the door behind her.

Immediately, she gagged and fought for breath. The air in the room was heavy with a dreadful, sickening stench.

Alice felt for a light switch.

"No . . ." she began, as the old, dirty lightbulb illuminated the scene in front of her. It was a bedroom, filled with old-fashioned furniture. But it was the bed that held her attention. Her hand came up to her mouth as she gagged in revulsion, her whole body shuddering at the hideous sight.

Lying side by side were two skeletons, their white-gray bones draped with shreds and strips of rotted clothing. A thousand screams howled in Alice's mind as she realized what she was looking at. The decaying garments were the same clothes worn by Mr. and Mrs. Wilkins.

At that moment, she was covered once again by a terrible chill. In the dull amber light, she watched in horror as Mr. and Mrs. Wilkins came *through* the closed door and into the bedroom. Alice fell backward — her body and senses numb with terror.

She screamed with everything left in her.

Mr. Wilkins put a finger to his smiling lips. "Shhh!" he hissed. "Don't wake the baby!"